Waves of power and danger had emanated from him and washed over her like some seductive potion.

Their eyes had met across the room and an electric current had zapped her down to her toes. Just like now.

The rough pad of his thumb trailed across her cheek and over her lips, which throbbed at his touch. She dropped her lashes, avoiding the fire in his eyes, afraid of getting scorched once again.

It didn't work.

His palm cradled the side of her head. His lips touched hers, and her bones melted.

She huffed out a breath against his mouth as she hooked an arm around his neck to stay vertical.

God help her. She'd fallen under his spell as quickly as she had in Zurich.

But now she had responsibilities. She planted her palms against his chest, and her fingers tingled to explore the hard slabs of muscle that shifted beneath his flannel shirt.

She pushed him away even as her lips kept contact with his.

CATCH, RELEASE

—

CAROL ERICSON

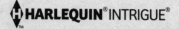

For all the strong women in my life
who keep it all together.

Recycling programs
for this product may
not exist in your area.

ISBN-13: 978-0-373-74779-5

CATCH, RELEASE

Copyright © 2013 by Carol Ericson

Printed in U.S.A.

ABOUT THE AUTHOR

Carol Ericson lives with her husband and two sons in Southern California, home of state-of-the-art cosmetic surgery, wild freeway chases, palm trees bending in the Santa Ana winds and a million amazing stories. These stories, along with hordes of virile men and feisty women, clamor for release from Carol's head. It makes for some interesting headaches until she sets them free to fulfill their destinies and her readers' fantasies. To find out more about Carol, her books and her strange headaches, please visit her website, www.carolericson.com, "where romance flirts with danger."

Books by Carol Ericson

HARLEQUIN INTRIGUE

*Brothers in Arms
***Guardians of Coral Cove
**Brothers in Arms: Fully Engaged

CAST OF CHARACTERS

Deb Sinclair—First female Prospero agent whose son has been kidnapped by international arms dealer Nico Zendaris. Now Zendaris is calling the shots and Deb has to follow his instructions to save her son, unless she can get help from an unlikely ally—her son's father.

Beau Slater—A covert ops gun for hire, Beau can't turn down a job from Prospero once he discovers the assignment is to track down rogue Prospero agent Deb Sinclair, the woman with whom he shared an unforgettable night three years ago.

Bobby Sinclair—Deb's kidnapped son has a serious illness, one that can be cured only by his father, the father he's never known.

Dr. Scott Herndon—This scientist and professor emeritus at MIT has something Deb needs to save her son, but will she be willing to kill him to get it?

Damon—Zendaris's henchman. He has his own plans for Deb...and they might just get her son killed.

Jack Coburn—The head of Prospero has two problems on his hands—one of his best agents may have gone rogue and the contractor he hires to find her has his own agenda.

Nico Zendaris—An international arms dealer who was burned by Prospero Team Three. Now he wants revenge and he's going to use Deb and her son to get it.

Chapter One

Deb's eye twitched along with her trigger finger, but she wasn't packing. They'd know. Somehow they knew everything, and they'd warned her if she didn't come alone and unarmed they'd hurt Bobby.

She believed them. Nico Zendaris had made good on every threat so far. Why would she start doubting him now?

Her gaze darted among the faces surging around the frosty Boston street corner. Would someone give her a sign? She clutched her cell phone in the pocket of her coat. She didn't know how they planned to contact her.

One if by land, two if by sea? She was in the right place for signals.

Someone bumped her and mumbled an apology. She stared at the stranger's back, his broad shoulders encased in a puffy down jacket, as he lumbered down the sidewalk. Was that the sign?

She took a few uncertain steps after him, but

he turned a corner and disappeared. Stumbling to a stop, she bit her lip. Should she go after him?

The message had ordered her to stand in this spot until further instructions. Was the bump an instruction? Or was the man just a clumsy pedestrian hurrying to his next appointment?

She no longer trusted her instincts since she'd allowed them to snatch Bobby. She should've known. She should've done more.

With a halting gait, she retraced her steps to the lamppost on the corner. If she did everything they asked of her, she'd get Bobby back. Zendaris had promised.

She ground her teeth against the sour bile rising from her gut. She knew better than to trust that man, but what choice did she have?

She'd have to trust him up to the moment he put a bullet in her head. Or she put one in his.

Her cell phone chirped, and she dragged it from her pocket with a hand shaking so badly she almost dropped the phone. She studied the blank display as the phone chirped again. She'd set her phone to vibrate.

She swiveled her head from side to side. Plenty of people with cell phones walked by, but nobody had stopped near her.

The phone chirped again. Gasping, she plunged her hand in her other coat pocket, her fingers colliding with another phone. Not hers.

She grabbed the cell and pulled it from her pocket. It continued its insistent trilling, so she hit the talk button.

"Hello?"

"Hello, Deb. For being a crack Prospero agent, it sure took you long enough to figure out you had a ringing phone in your pocket."

The smooth mocking voice stirred her blood, thick with rage. "That was one of your little minions who bumped into me?"

He chuckled. "Very astute of you—finally."

She didn't even know if the man on the phone was Zendaris. She'd never heard his voice even though Prospero Team Three had disrupted one of his biggest arms deals four years ago.

She growled low in her throat. "I should've dropped him in his tracks."

"Tough talk from the first and only female Prospero agent." He clicked his tongue. "But you wouldn't do that now, would you, Deb? Not while we have Bobby."

His words twisted a knife in her belly and she bit back a sob. She refused to show this scum any sign of weakness. "Let me talk to him. I'm not going to do anything more until you do. I have to know he's okay."

"Deb, Deb, Deb. He's not with me, or I'd gladly put him on the phone. Rest assured he's safe and comfortable. We'll give you proof of life soon enough."

His phrase *proof of life* had her sagging against the lamppost. He'd better show her proof of Bobby's life, or she'd hand Zendaris proof of his own death.

"When? I need something now."

"You have my word, Deb. That's all I can give you at the present time—that and the phone you're using."

She had an urge to toss the thing and the slick voice coming from it into oncoming traffic. But it represented her only connection to Bobby.

She crushed it against her ear. "What's the significance of this phone?"

"It will be our way of communicating with you. It's secure, untraceable, a very special phone. Carry it with you everywhere."

"So what is it, Zendaris? If that's who you really are." Despite the chill in the air, sweat dampened her hairline. She brushed a bead of it away. "What do you want me to do?"

"You Americans, so impatient. You just keep the phone by your side, Deb, and we'll tell you what to do next."

"Why the delay? Tell me what to do now so we can end this game." Silence greeted her plea and she was almost glad of it. A whining, desperate tone had crept into her voice—a tone she didn't want Zendaris to hear.

She examined the phone and pushed a few buttons. There were no contacts, no phone numbers appeared and it didn't seem as if she could make an outgoing call. What other special features did it have? A GPS tracking device? A camera? Were they watching her right now?

Closing her eyes, she rested her forehead against the cold metal of the lamppost and dropped the phone in her coat pocket. What was Zendaris after? What did he want her to do?

She swallowed. Why was she kidding herself? He wanted the plans to the anti-drone. He'd had them first, lost them to her Prospero teammate, Cade Stark, and then the plans had been stolen from Cade.

Neither Zendaris nor Prospero knew the location of the plans, but he must think she knew something. Or he planned to use her to get them.

The phone rang again. That was fast. Now maybe they could get down to business.

"What?"

A different voice greeted her this time, rougher, gruffer. "Face east and take the first right."

She spun around to face the right direction. "Where the man who dropped the phone in my pocket went?"

"Do it."

With the phone clamped to her ear, she strode to the next corner and turned. "What now?"

"Walk two blocks and turn down the alley after the green awning."

She spied a flower shop with a green awning in front and aimed her steps toward it. The man on the other end of the line said nothing, but his heavy breathing kept her moving.

Would they show her some sign that Bobby was okay? Maybe Bobby was down that alley. The thought quickened her steps.

She stopped at the entrance to the alley and braced her hand against the corner of the flower shop building. Her gaze tracked along the length of the alley, stumbling over two Dumpsters but nothing else. No Bobby.

Her shoulders slumped. "I'm in the alley."

"Go to the second Dumpster and take out the black bag."

Her stomach tightened into knots as she crept down the pavement, avoiding the patches of ice that the winter sun hadn't melted. She didn't want to look into that Dumpster. Didn't want to look into any bag.

Fear had her in its grip. Even though she hadn't been acting like it, she was a trained Prospero agent, programmed to laugh in the face of fear.

Without cracking a smile, she pushed up the green lid of the second Dumpster with the heel of her hand. She peered inside and eyed a black duffel bag sitting atop bags of trash and stems, leaves and broken blooms from the flower shop. She gagged at the stench of rotting organic material.

Holding her breath, she balanced one foot on the wheel of the Dumpster and hoisted herself up. She reached into the refuse and snagged the strap of the bag and pulled. It didn't budge.

"I have to put the phone down."

The man grunted in response, and she slid the phone in her pocket. Using both hands, she propelled herself farther into the Dumpster, grabbed the bag with both hands and hauled it out.

She dropped the heavy prize on the ground and crouched beside it. She dipped her hand in her pocket and retrieved the phone. "I have the bag. Should I open it?"

"Yeah, whaddya think?"

She thought if she made one wrong move they'd harm Bobby. It took her two tries to unzip the bag with her trembling hands. When the bag gaped open, she sat back on her heels, her mouth as wide as the opening of the duffel.

"What am I supposed to do with this stuff?"

"Rob a jewelry store."

The shock made her giggle and she toppled over. She sniffed and rubbed her eyes. "What are you talking about?"

"You're robbing a jewelry store. It's a few blocks away."

"Are you crazy? This is what Zendaris wants me to do? Steal some jewels?"

He ignored her questions and began giving her instructions for the robbery. He stopped after every instruction and asked her if she understood. She'd had him repeat the first few directions as the fog slowly cleared from her mind.

Zendaris was serious. He wanted her to rob a store. She knew the consequences if she didn't do it. Was this it? Was this all he'd ask of her?

She might get killed in the attempt, and if she were arrested she would never reveal her motivation. She understood what that would mean for Bobby.

"You got all that?"

"Yes."

"Don't fail."

"I don't plan on it."

She cleared out her own purse and dumped the contents into the big designer bag that was stuffed in the duffel. She pulled the blond wig over her head and clapped the huge sunglasses on her face.

While sitting on the ground with her back against the Dumpster, Deb slipped a pair of high heels onto her feet. Zendaris had told her to dress professionally. The towering heels must've been an afterthought and were more suited to a hooker than the low heels she'd kicked off, but they added to her disguise.

Peering into the mirror Zendaris had thoughtfully provided, she shoved the dark strands of her hair beneath the wig and applied red lipstick.

She crammed the black ski mask into the purse as well, and then tucked the loaded .45 inside—not that she planned on shooting anyone unless Zendaris showed up in the jewelry store.

She pushed to her feet and dropped the duffel bag along with her own empty purse into the Dumpster. She'd put her shoes and everything else from her purse into the designer bag. She tightened the belt of her wool coat and emerged from the alley a new woman.

Maybe blondes did have more fun. A few men cast assessing glances her way as she wobbled down the sidewalk in her high heels.

She passed by the jewelry store once and waited until the lone customer had left. Then she approached the door and stabbed the buzzer. They must've liked what they saw because the door clicked and she pushed through with butterflies taking flight in her belly.

Two clerks. Deb smiled. In her affected Southern accent, she said, "Ahm lookin' for a diamond bracelet?"

One of the clerks, probably a jeweler, looked

up from poking at something on a glass table. The magnifying contraption he wore on his head enlarged his eye and Deb felt as if he were staring right through her disguise.

He went back to his work, and the female clerk crossed the room to a velvet-lined case. "We have some beautiful bracelets over here."

"Perfect."

While the clerk bent over the case to unlock it, Deb stepped back and locked the door to the shop, flipping the sign to Closed. She withdrew the gun from her purse as she yanked on the cord to the blinds.

"Excuse me?" The noises had caught the attention of the jeweler and he looked up with his hideously magnified eye.

Before turning around, Deb pulled the ski mask over her head, blond hair and everything, and swung the gun toward him. "Ahm sorry, sir, ahm goin' to have to ask you to move away from the counter."

He dropped his hand from the top of the counter and Deb aimed the gun at his head. "Please don't."

The clerk stood with her mouth open, holding a tray of bracelets in front of her.

"We'll start with those."

While the jeweler kneeled in the middle of the store with his hands behind his head, Deb had the clerk scurrying around the store dumping trays of jewels into her big bag.

Deb apologized repeatedly, but she knew these people would be traumatized. If she could make it up to them one day, she would.

Zendaris never told her how much to steal, so with the bag bulging and half the cases empty, Deb held up her hand. "That's enough. Both of you in the back room. Ahm not goin' to hurt y'all."

She herded them into the back office, which Zendaris had known about. She'd already collected their cell phones, and now she ripped the desk phone out of the wall and smashed it.

"Ahm goin' to lock you in here now, but you should be able to get out soon."

She slammed the door shut and dragged a chair over to wedge it beneath the doorknob. That should hold them until she got away. If she got away.

She pulled the ski mask from her head, shook out her blond hair and replaced her sunglasses. Hoisting the bag with the loot over her shoulder, she slipped from the store, keeping it locked behind her.

Her heels clicked down the sidewalk as she clutched a key chain in her hand and made for the corner. She let out a breath when she saw a blue compact car parked at a meter.

The remote Zendaris had included in the duffel unlocked the car and she slipped inside, her heart pounding unsteadily. She adjusted the rearview mirror and brushed the blond locks from her sweaty brow.

Deb pulled away from the curb. Nice and easy. No hurry. No cops were on her tail. No sirens wailed in her wake.

What did Zendaris want her to do with the jewelry? He didn't need it. Didn't want it. He just wanted her—her total submission. He had that. As long as he had Bobby.

But when she got out of this mess, Zendaris would pay. Unless she wound up dead or in jail.

Following the instructions to a T, she drove across the bridge to Cambridge and pulled into the parking lot of a hotel. She hadn't noticed any cops following her, although she'd seen a couple of possible tails and had lost them.

Maybe Zendaris's guys making sure she got to her destination.

She tilted the mirror down and fluffed up the wig. Then she wiped the lipstick from her mouth with a tissue. Not her color.

Checking in was a breeze with her fake ID and the cash Zendaris had provided.

She hitched the bag stuffed with jewels over her shoulder and made a beeline for the elevator.

Once inside, she slumped against the wall and closed her eyes.

What did he have planned for her next? She'd see the fear in that poor jewelry store clerk's eyes before she fell asleep tonight.

When the elevator jostled to a stop on her floor, Deb stepped through the doors and wandered down the hallway looking for her room. A couple passed her, arguing on their way to the elevator, and a maid emerged from one of the rooms.

Deb turned a corner and located her room number. She slid the key card in and out. Red lights blinked at her. She tried again and grasped the handle, bracing her hip against the heavy door.

A soft footfall sounded behind her on the dense carpet. She turned her head to the side. But she was too late.

Something hard and unforgiving prodded the small of her back, and a hoarse whisper grated against her ear.

"Keep moving into the room…and maybe I won't kill you."

Chapter Two

Deb marched in front of him, her long blond hair swaying against her stiff back.

She looked better as a redhead.

"Drop the bag and the coat, and pin your shoulders to the wall next to the bed."

She swung around, her green eyes wide and shooting sparks. "You!"

"Do it, Deb. Right against the wall, and don't try any funny business or you'll be eating carpet."

Her bag and coat fell to the floor. Two red spots formed on her cheeks and her hands clenched into fists, but she backed up to the wall, nearly stumbling in those ridiculously high heels. Who robbed a jewelry store in stilettos?

She lined up against the wall, tucking her hands behind her back. "What are you doing here?"

Beau held up his hand—the one without the

gun. "Spread your legs and put your arms out to your sides."

Her nostrils flared, and he could almost see the steam coming out of them.

She widened her stance and flattened her palms against the wall. "I'm not carrying."

"That would be a first."

"The gun's in that pretty designer bag on the floor."

He raised his brows. "At least you're honest." He took one step back and kicked the bag toward the open bathroom door.

With his weapon still trained on Deb, he reached out and ran his hand down one side of her body and then the other. He lightly cupped each of her breasts, and then slid his hand beneath her straight skirt.

The last time they'd done this it had been a lot more pleasant.

He whipped a plastic tie from his back pocket and twirled his finger in the air. "Turn around and place your hands behind your back."

She complied and he grabbed her wrists with one hand, dragging his gaze away from her rounded derriere. He hadn't bothered to tell Prospero that he'd met Deb before, but he knew he wouldn't let this get personal. He always kept things professional—until the night he'd met her.

Once he had a firm grasp on her arm, he

placed his weapon on the bed and cinched the plastic tie around her wrists. He retrieved his weapon and pulled her toward the bed until the back of her knees met the mattress. "Sit."

She dropped to the bed, and her skirt hiked up around her thighs.

Beau shoved his gun in the back of his waistband and yanked down the hem of her skirt. *Keep it professional.*

"Start talking. Why are you in contact with Zendaris and why did you just rob that jewelry store? I'm assuming one is connected to the other."

Her lush lips formed a stubborn line. "So Prospero hired Loki to track me down?"

A muscle in his jaw twitched when she used his code name. He never had told her his real name—even after the night of passion they'd shared.

"Prospero hires the best." He hunched forward, bracing his hands on his knees. "What the hell are you doing, Deb? How did Zendaris get you, of all people, to turn?"

She scooted back on the bed, and her breasts strained against the silky material of her blouse. Her jaw tightened and her eyes narrowed—green cat eyes. They'd captivated him from the moment he'd met her at that gathering of world leaders in Zurich.

He cleared his throat. "Don't think I'm just going to turn you over to the Boston P.D. for that armed robbery. I'm working for Prospero. You do know what Prospero does to traitors, don't you?"

Her Adam's apple bobbed in the delicate column of her throat. "They wouldn't… Jack would never…"

He sliced his hand through the air and straightened to his full height. "Jack Coburn will do whatever necessary to protect the security and interests of this country."

Sniffling, she turned her head away, tucking her cheek against her shoulder.

He'd brought Deb Sinclair to tears? That had to be a first. He'd had her moaning in his arms for one night, but nobody had ever made the first female Prospero agent cry.

Of course, it could all be a ruse.

He grabbed the silky blond strands of the wig and yanked it off her head. Her own dark auburn hair tumbled to her shoulders, catching the sunlight that flooded the room through the open curtains.

"Why'd you do it?"

She puckered her lips and blew at a few strands of hair clinging to her lips. "What are they paying you? I'll give you half of my haul."

Beau reached forward and she flinched,

squeezing her eyes shut. Did she really think he'd hit her?

He brushed the hair from her face, his palm making contact with her smooth skin. He snatched his hand away before the gesture turned into a caress.

Why in the hell did he think he could keep this impersonal? That night with Deb had rocked his world. He'd never forgotten it, or her.

"Make this easy on yourself, Deb. Was it money? I know you never had much growing up. Jack might even understand that motivation. Come clean and give them what you have on Zendaris."

A little smile played across her mouth. "You never told them, did you?"

Warmth burned in his chest and he crossed his arms. "This isn't about me. You're the one with a bag full of stolen jewels."

She threw back her head and laughed so hard her shoulders shook. She fell back on the bed and laughed at the ceiling until tears rolled into her ears.

When she sat up, little black streaks smudged her cheeks. "Loki never told Prospero he bedded the prey, did he?"

"It's irrelevant." Beau ground his teeth together, knowing damned well it wasn't irrelevant.

"Right." She wrinkled her nose and sniffed.

"I'm sure Jack wouldn't have hired the great Loki if he'd known his assassin had already gotten intimate with the target."

"That was a long time ago, and I agreed to take the assignment before I knew you were the quarry."

"But once you found out I was the...quarry... you should've come clean. Don't you think so, Loki?" She blinked and raised one dark eyebrow. "I bet you enjoyed that pat-down. Did it bring back fond memories?"

Her emerald gaze dropped below his belt. "Did it excite you?"

He turned his back on her with the blood running hot in his veins. He snagged the purse by the handle and dumped its contents on the carpet at Deb's feet.

The .45 thudded to the floor—not Deb's usual weapon. As he recalled, she preferred a Glock. Shoes tumbled out along with a ski mask and a tangle of jewelry.

Why would she want this stuff? She'd had a tough life as a kid. Maybe this satisfied some deep psychological need within her. And what did it all have to do with Zendaris?

Could Prospero be wrong? There had been the slimmest of leads linking Deb to Zendaris—that and the fact that she'd dropped below the radar.

Maybe her behavior signaled some kind of

breakdown and not a traitorous move to Zen-daris's camp.

He ran his fingers through the gems. "Why'd you steal this jewelry, Deb?"

She shrugged and the top button of her blouse popped open. "I wanted it."

"Why are you in contact with Zendaris?" *Come on, Deb. Just deny it.*

Yawning, she flopped back onto the bed.

He drove his fist into the pile of jewelry and hopped onto the bed, his knees straddling her hips, his hands on either side of her head. "Tell me what's going on."

She dropped her dark lashes, still long and lush without the mascara her tears of laughter had washed away. "I'm not telling you anything."

He blew out an exasperated breath, which stirred the tendrils of her hair at her forehead. "I'm taking you in, Deb."

Her body stiffened beneath him, and her eyes flew open. "T-to Prospero?"

"You're their monster. They can deal with you."

She bit her bottom lip but not before he saw it tremble.

"I'll tell them everything, Loki. I'll tell them how you seduced me that night when you were supposed to be guarding the emir's wife."

"Ooh, and you promised you wouldn't kiss and tell."

"I mean it. I'll tell them how we made love all night long and while you were lying there, sated and naked and conked out, I went through your things. You compromised your position and the security of the people you were supposed to be protecting."

And I'd do it all again for one more night with you.

He stared into her eyes, bright with unshed tears. "It's your word against mine, Deb."

"I—I'll ruin your reputation. I'll destroy you."

Tough words, but her voice quavered and cracked when she delivered them.

"Maybe I don't care. Maybe it's time for Loki to die anyway."

She squirmed beneath him and started to bend one of her knees for a well-aimed shot between his legs.

He dropped on top of her, pressing his frame along every line of hers as she huffed out a sigh. Her soft breasts smooshed against his chest. Her sweet scent invaded his pores.

He wanted her, even now. He wanted her traitorous lips against his. He wanted to take her lying tongue into his mouth. He wanted her deceiving hands on his body.

She thrashed from side to side. It only inflamed his desire.

He rolled from her body and stood by the side of the bed, hovering over her. "Sit up."

"That's what I was trying to do before you pinned me."

"You were trying to knee me in the groin."

"A girl has to protect herself." She struggled to a sitting position. "You'd better think long and hard about turning me in, Loki. I'll bring you down with me."

"What I did was child's play compared to your crimes." He put more distance between them and her sweet scent that lured him to craziness. "Besides, your reputation will be so sullied, I can claim that you seduced and drugged me. Why not? Two can play hardball, sweetheart."

"I don't want to play hardball."

She fluttered her eyelashes in an amateur attempt at flirtation, which fell flat. The Deb Sinclair he knew didn't flirt like some simpering college girl. The Deb Sinclair he knew flirted like a woman—bold, challenging, sexy as hell.

"Let me go, Loki. Stealing a few jewels is not endangering national security. Besides, what do you care about that? You've always gone to the highest bidder and damn the torpedoes."

"I think those claims about me have been

greatly exaggerated—maybe even by me. Prospero hired me to do a job, and I'm going to do it. This is Jack Coburn we're talking about. Nobody betrays Jack Coburn, and you're about to find out why."

"He doesn't have to know." She lifted her shoulder to rub the edge of her jaw against it. "Tell him I got away, that you couldn't find me at all. I'm a Prospero agent. That won't be too hard for him to believe."

"And I'm Loki. It'll be hard to believe I didn't run you to ground."

"Nice analogy." She closed her eyes and heaved out a sigh. "Please. I'm begging you. Th-this is not what it seems. Somebody's life depends on this—on my betrayal or at least the appearance of my betrayal."

Narrowing his eyes, he rubbed his knuckles against the stubble on his chin. She'd shifted tactics. "Your life? Zendaris has threatened to kill the members of Prospero Team Three several times over. He's never gotten the chance."

"Not my life. Much worse than that."

He and Deb had not only had an intense physical connection that night three years ago. When they weren't exploring each other's bodies, they were exploring each other's minds. She'd told him the only family she'd had was the old man who had taken her in as a rebellious teen. Was Zendaris threatening him?

"Your foster father?"

"Robert died last year." A single tear rolled down her cheek, and his heart lurched.

Was she playing him?

He set his jaw and shoved his hands in his pockets. "Sorry to hear it, but if not Robert, who? You told me you had no family other than Robert."

She jerked her head up. "You remembered that?"

He remembered every detail of that night—the musky scent of her perfume, the smooth curves of her body, the low throatiness of her laugh and the taste of her. Sometimes at night that taste still lingered on his tongue.

He squared his shoulders. "I do, so don't try to play some sob story off on me."

"It's not a story, Loki. Zendaris is holding someone I love more than life itself."

A knife twisted in his gut—a husband. Deb had gotten married. And why not? Their connection had been almost three years ago—a one-night stand. Why would that mean anything to her?

He nodded. "You're married."

"No." She shook her head from side to side so vehemently that her hair slipped over one shoulder and then the other. "I'm not talking about a husband. I'm talking about my son. Zendaris kidnapped my son, Bobby. And if I don't do exactly what he tells me to do, he'll kill him."

Chapter Three

Much worse than a husband. Husbands could disappear. Kids stayed with you forever.

That one-night stand had meant less to her than he thought. She must've left him and run to the arms of some other lover.

Unless she was lying. What better way to get off the hook than to play the kid card?

His sharp laugh cut through the confusion. "You're good, Deb. I have to give you that. You're a pro."

"Can you unbind my wrists?" She raised her arms behind her. "I didn't expect you to believe me…at first."

He strolled to the minibar and snatched a bottle of water from the fridge. He downed half of it in one gulp. He didn't want her to see that she'd gotten to him for a minute.

"Unbind you so you can go for your gun? Claw my face off? Make a run for it?"

Her mouth curved up on one side. "You're Loki. I'm not going anywhere. We both know that."

"I'm impervious to flattery."

"Since when?" She tipped her chin at the floor where he'd scattered the contents of her bag. "Then get my wallet. I have a picture of my son."

He wished she'd stop saying that—it sounded so permanent. He slammed the plastic bottle on the credenza. Swooping down, he scooped up the wallet and flipped to the plastic inserts.

A teenaged Deb smiled at him, leaning over a chair, her arms around a grizzled African-American man—Robert, the man who'd taken her in after she'd run away from foster care. He flipped to the next picture and froze.

A towheaded toddler grinned while clutching the handlebars of a red tricycle. He flicked the edge of the picture. The kid didn't even look like her. "This doesn't prove anything."

"Why would I carry a picture of a boy in my wallet? You know I don't have any family, no nephews."

"Doesn't prove anything. Some wallets come with pictures already inserted. Is he even yours?"

"Look at the next picture."

He swallowed as he stared at Deb wearing a hospital gown and cradling a baby. She looked… happy. "Congratulations. I'm sorry for doubting you. It looks like you really do have a child, but there's nothing here to convince me Zendaris has him."

"Well, at least you admitted I'm his mother. Zendaris has him. I'm telling the truth, Loki."

"Stop—" he dropped the wallet on the bed next to her "—calling me that."

"But I don't know your real name. You never told me your real name." She sniffled and her nose reddened.

She was sucking him in again. How was she playing the victim when she hadn't wasted any time replacing him in her bed? Hell, she could've had a boyfriend when they'd hooked up.

If she'd lied about that, how did he know any of this story was true? The picture proved Deb had given birth, but for all he knew the boy could be safe with his father.

"Where is his father?"

She waved her hands. "Out of the picture."

His pulse leapt. At least that was a plus. "I'm sorry if any of this is true, Deb. But if Zendaris has your son, you need to contact Prospero."

Her shoulders sagged. "If I contact Prospero, Zendaris will kill him. You know he tried to do the same thing to one of my team members. He tried to kidnap Cade's son, but Cade was able to protect his son."

The tears ran unabated down her cheeks, and they were just about enough to convince Beau that her story was true. Nobody could fake the anguish he read in her face. And Deb Sinclair didn't cry.

He secured his weapon and hers and sank onto the bed next to her. Reaching behind her back, he released her wrists.

She put her hands in her lap and rubbed the red creases on her skin, but the crying continued.

Slipping an arm around her shoulder, he pulled her flush against his side. Her head dropped to the hollow of his shoulder.

It felt good. He felt good.

"I'm sorry." She rubbed her nose. "I don't think I've cried since the day they snatched him. What's the use of tears?"

She'd discovered early in life that tears didn't solve anything. At least her crying seemed to soften Loki's position.

And she hadn't even had to tell him Bobby was his son.

When she'd heard his voice growl in her ear, hope and fear immediately began to war in her brain. Hope that Loki could help her, especially once she told him Zendaris had his son, too, and fear that he wouldn't believe her and drag her back to Prospero.

If he did that, Bobby would die.

Now was not the time to tell him he had a son. How could she prove to him that Bobby was his anyway? The timing alone wouldn't work. They'd had a one-night stand, and as incredible as it had been for her, he'd had no idea if she'd had a boyfriend or even a husband at that time. Just as she'd had no idea if he'd had a girlfriend or wife. Might even have one now.

He squeezed her closer. "Tell me what happened. How'd Zendaris get Bobby and what does he want? Not someone to rob jewelry stores for him?"

Deb smothered a hiccup with her hand. "One of his thugs impersonated Robert and kidnapped Bobby from daycare. After Robert's death, I stupidly left him on the approved guardian list. When the man claiming to be Robert came to the daycare with ID, they released my son to him."

She crossed her arms across her stomach. Whenever she went back to that day, she got physically ill.

"How long ago was this?"

"Almost a week ago."

"You didn't do a very good job of playing it cool. That's exactly when Prospero pegged your unusual behavior. A little more digging and it was enough for them to call me in."

"I couldn't tell Prospero, couldn't tell Jack. Zendaris warned me that if I called in the police or Prospero, he'd kill Bobby." She ended on a sob despite her efforts to stop the waterworks.

"How did he contact you?"

"He left me a note at the daycare." She pointed to the wallet. "May I?"

Loki may have offered her a shoulder to lean on, but his lean muscles were still coiled as if on high alert. She didn't want to give him any reason to shoot her.

He nodded and she reached for the wallet. She plucked a folded piece of paper from the billfold and smoothed it out on her thigh. "The pretend Robert left this when he took Bobby."

Leaning over, he read it aloud. "'We have your son. If you call the police or notify Prospero, he's dead.'"

He cursed and jumped up from the bed. "And you knew right away it was Zendaris?"

"Of course. Who else? He'd been trying to get to us through our families for years."

He stopped suddenly and spun around. "How did Robert die?"

"He had a heart attack."

"Are you sure? Heart attacks can be induced."

"Robert had already had one heart attack. His death wasn't completely unexpected."

Shoving his hands in his pockets, he paced in front of the window. "What did they do next? How did they contact you?"

"They sent me another note with instructions to come to Boston, dress a certain way and stand on a busy street corner. While I was waiting, someone bumped into me and slipped a phone in my pocket. Zendaris, or whoever, called me on that phone and told me the plan for the jewelry store robbery."

"Where's the phone now?"

"In the pocket of the coat I dropped by the door."

He picked up the crumpled black coat and shoved his hand in the pocket.

She jumped up, waving her hands. "Don't make any calls on it. It's a special phone."

"Have you looked at this thing yet?" He turned it over and brought it close to his face. "How do you know it's not bugged with a mic or a camera or a GPS?"

She covered her mouth with her hands. That had flashed across her mind before, but she hadn't found the opportunity to examine the phone. If it had been recording everything she said, she'd just killed Bobby.

In two steps, she was at Loki's side. "I didn't even look. I didn't even think. If Prospero could see me now, they'd fire me for incompetence."

"I think they'd excuse you under the circumstances." He squinted at the back of the phone and rubbed his thumb across it. "I don't see anything that would indicate a camera or a mic, but a GPS is a strong possibility. Did Zendaris tell you what he wanted you to do with the jewelry?"

"No. I don't even understand why he wanted me to hit that store."

"Control."

Deb swallowed and knotted her fingers in front of her as she stepped back from Loki. "I sort of figured that."

"He wants to see how far you'll go to save your son." He slammed the phone against his palm. "What does he really want from you?"

"He wants the plans to the anti-drone."

"The anti-drone? Is that what I think it is?"

"A team of scientists and engineers worked on a weapon to neutralize our fleet of drones. They came up with a set of plans for a prototype and one of our agents stole them. Within a few days, they were stolen from him—from someone inside our organization. Nobody knows where they are now, but Zendaris must think I do or at least he thinks he can use me to find them."

"Then we'd better start thinking of a plan that's going to make him believe you can do it while we work on finding Bobby."

"We?" She spun around with her arms out-stretched. "You're going to help me, Loki?"

"Only if you stop calling me that ridiculous code name."

"I'd love to, except that night we didn't get around to proper introductions."

His mouth quirked. "There was nothing proper about that night at all."

Her blood stirred. Did he still think about it the way she did? Did he lie awake some nights and relive every sensation?

Of course, she'd had a living reminder of their night together in the form of Bobby. And she didn't regret one minute of it, then or now.

She thrust out her hand. "I'm Deb Sinclair. It's a pleasure to meet you."

He took her hand. She'd expected a firm handshake, but his long fingers almost caressed her wrist as he brushed his palm against hers.

"Beau Slater, and the pleasure is all mine."

"Beau." The name puffed from her lips. *Bobby Slater.* It worked. "Why are you helping me, Beau Slater? What's in it for you?"

She had to admit to herself that when she'd first heard his voice, she'd immediately thought she could get him to help her by revealing the truth about Bobby's parentage. A cheap shot, but she wasn't above cheap shots to save Bobby. But he'd offered to help without even knowing.

Why?

"If I haul you back to Prospero, that's not going to get anyone any closer to Zendaris. If you're in contact with him, that's a big step."

She narrowed her eyes. Self-interest—she could believe that. "Has anyone ever sent you on Zendaris's trail?"

"Yes—" he tossed the phone onto the bed "—but I'm not at liberty to reveal the identity of my employer, even now."

"It wasn't the U.S. government, was it?"

He drew a line across his lips. "Not telling. Of course, if you went to Prospero and told Jack Coburn everything you just told me, he'd believe you and probably want to use you as bait."

"No!"

"What about your team members? I know how Prospero works—teams of four agents. Let them in on it. They could help you."

"Are you afraid you're not up to the job?"

His gaze wandered lazily down her body, from her face to the tips of her toes. "Oh, I'm up for the job. I'm just curious why you wouldn't bring your team in on this. Makes me wonder if everything you've told me is the truth."

How could she explain to him her inability to trust her teammates? She had such high regard for them and would help them in a second, but she couldn't dismiss the fact that they were all highly trained professionals—men who wanted nothing more than to get their hands on Zendaris and those plans.

Would they really let a little boy stand between

them and those goals? Because if it came down to it, she'd turn over those plans and let Zendaris escape if it meant keeping Bobby safe.

"Everything I told you is the truth." Except for the fact that he was Bobby's father.

"It seems strange, like something's off. I probably should just do my job and deliver you to Prospero."

She straightened her spine and widened her stance. "I'm not going in without a fight."

A fierce light exploded in his blue eyes. Then he lunged at her and tackled her to the floor.

Chapter Four

He was insane. Bobby's father had gone over the edge. But then, what had she ever really known about him?

For the second time since he'd bulldozed back into her life, he had her pinned with his body—and it wasn't as pleasurable as the first time he'd done it three years ago.

"Get off me." She shoved at his chest, which might as well have been crafted from stone. "Are you going to hog-tie me and carry me back? I'm not going anywhere with you."

His heart pounded against her chest, his breath ragged in her hair. His voice rasped. "Stay here."

He rolled from her body and began an army crawl toward the window.

He didn't plan to kill her after all, or haul her back to Prospero—at least not right this minute. She dragged a few breaths of air into her lungs and brought her knees to her chest, rocking forward.

He stopped his crawl and whipped his head around. "Stay down."

"Why? What are you doing?"

"Someone just tried to shoot you."

"What?" She wrapped her arms around her legs, curling into a fetal position.

Beau shimmied to the drapes and yanked them across the windows from the bottom. "Crawl to the bathroom."

Her mouth so dry she couldn't peel her tongue from the roof, Deb mimicked Beau's army crawl until she hit the cold tile of the bathroom floor. Grasping the edge of the tub, she pulled herself onto its edge.

A few seconds later, Beau joined her. He wedged his backside against the vanity and crossed his arms. "What the hell is going on?"

"You're asking me?" The squeak in her voice echoed in the small space. "How do you know someone was trying to shoot me?"

"You had a red laser beam right here." He planted the tip of his index finger in the middle of his forehead.

She gasped and her body sagged. She clutched the edge of the tub to stop her slide into it. "Someone had a scope on me?"

"Well, I don't think it was a light show."

"Did you see anything out the window?"

"I wasn't looking, but there's a building across the way. It must've come from there."

She hoisted herself from the tub and flattened her hands on the vanity, leaning toward the mirror. "It couldn't be Zendaris. That doesn't make any sense. Why would he kill me before putting me to work?"

"My question exactly." Beau turned to face the mirror and caught the eye of her reflection. "Unless he knows I'm here and he's putting the brakes on his plan."

"God, I hope not. If he thinks I called someone in to help me, he'll kill Bobby—before he kills me."

Beau ran a hand up her spine and clasped the back of her neck. "Let's not think the worst. Do you have any way to contact him? The phone?"

"That's a one-way phone. I can't call out on it."

"Who would be after you?"

She met his blue gaze in the mirror and swallowed hard. "Prospero."

"Prospero hired me."

She shrugged away from him and returned to the tub, gripping the plastic shower curtain with one hand. "Maybe Prospero hired two Lokis— one to reel in the catch and one to gut her."

He raised an eyebrow. "If that were the plan, I would've left you in range of the little red dot on your forehead instead of pushing you down."

"Maybe Prospero is using you." She shoved the shower curtain away from her and the silver rings clattered on the rod. "Do you really think Jack Coburn isn't aware that we slept together? He knew all along. That's why he hired you. He figured you were the best person to find me. Figured I might just trust you instead of running away...or killing you."

"I hope he's right." He hooked a thumb in his pocket and a crooked grin played across his face.

"I fail to see the humor." She shoved her hands in her hair, letting it run through her fingers and fall about her shoulders.

"Coburn wouldn't order your execution without listening to what you had to say first. My assignment was to find you and bring you in."

"That was *your* mission." Her gaze tracked to the open bathroom door. "Maybe he gave someone else different orders."

He pushed off the vanity and grabbed her hand. "I think you're looking in the wrong direction, Deb. Prospero doesn't want you dead."

"Someone does, and it's not Zendaris—at least not yet."

"We're getting out of here." He squeezed her hand. "Check out and we'll find another place."

"B-but I'm not supposed to leave."

"Do you think Zendaris would rather have you

dead? He has you exactly where he wants you. He's not going to squander this opportunity."

She chewed the inside of her lip. "What if it's all a game? What if Zendaris doesn't even care about those plans? He kidnapped Bobby and now he's torturing me. He has a personal vendetta against us, you know."

"Prospero?"

"Prospero Team Three specifically. One of our members recently discovered that Zendaris's wife may have been a casualty of the raid we conducted on one of his munitions factories. He blames us for killing his wife."

Beau whistled through his teeth. "That puts a different spin on this."

"Exactly. He wants revenge. What better way than to kidnap my son and then toy with me before…before he kills us both."

Beau pulled her against his chest, wrapping both of his strong arms around her. "That's not going to happen. I'm not going to let it happen."

"Why are you helping me, Beau?" She rubbed her nose against the soft flannel of his shirt. "Is it really just to get a crack at Zendaris?"

"That and I have a soft spot for…kids." He tilted her head up with a finger beneath her chin. "Do you take me for some kind of coldhearted killer?"

She blinked her eyes. "I'd heard about you before I ran into you that night in Zurich—the mysterious Loki, Norse god of mischief. I knew all the stories—the hostage rescue in Mali, boarding that Somali pirate ship, taking down the mastermind behind that string of embassy bombings in London, the assassinations."

He put a finger against her lips. "Didn't happen."

"If you say so." She shrugged. She'd been half in love with Loki before she'd ever set eyes on him in the hotel bar where she'd been gathering intelligence at a conference of oil-producing nations.

Of course, she hadn't known the man of steel with the cobalt-blue eyes sipping scotch at the end of the mahogany bar was Loki in the flesh. But on some level, she'd sensed it. Waves of power and danger had emanated from him and washed over her like some seductive potion.

Their eyes met across the room and an electric current had zapped her down to her toes. Just like now.

The rough pad of his thumb trailed across her cheek and over her lips, which throbbed at his touch. She dropped her lashes, avoiding the fire in his eyes, afraid of getting scorched once again.

It didn't work.

His palm cradled the side of her head. His lips touched hers, and her bones melted.

She huffed out a breath against his mouth as she hooked an arm around his neck to stay vertical.

He deepened the kiss, slanting his mouth across hers, sliding his tongue between her teeth.

God help her. She'd bed him as quickly as she had in Zurich. He could have her right here on the bathroom floor and she'd welcome any discomfort, any inconvenience to have him inside her again.

But now she had responsibilities. She planted her palms against his chest, and her fingers tingled to explore the hard slabs of muscle that shifted beneath his flannel shirt.

She pushed him away even as her lips kept contact with his.

Despite her mixed messages, he got the hint and stepped back, ending their heated kiss. He cleared his throat. "Sorry."

"Me, too." She put a hand over her mouth as if to remove the temptation. "It just felt kind of good to share my burden, you know?"

Of course, sharing her burden didn't mean winding up in bed with the first man to offer his help. Not that Loki was just some man. He'd been *the* man for the past three years of her life.

"Let's get out of here." He dropped to the floor again. "I'm going to get that wig for you. Wear it out of here. We're going to have to take the car

Zendaris provided or he'll wonder how you're getting around."

"It's parked in the hotel parking lot. Where are we going?"

"Another hotel, but we'll stay in Cambridge just so you can show good faith to Zendaris. We don't want him to think you're trying to escape."

"What if that sniper was a test? What if he wants me to stay put no matter what happens?"

"Even Zendaris is not going to expect you to put yourself in mortal danger. He wouldn't trust someone like that to find the anti-drone plans."

Beau crawled back across the floor and swept the blond wig from the bed along with the phone and dragged the designer bag over the carpet. Once back in the bathroom, he shoved them at her.

"Here you go."

She tucked her hair beneath the wig, punched her arms into the sleeves of the coat and slung the heavy bag over her shoulder. "I'm ready."

Beau poked his head into the hallway and then gestured her through the door. Placing a hand against the small of her back, he guided her toward the stairwell. "Can you navigate the stairs in those shoes? I don't want to be a sitting duck in the elevator."

She kicked off the shoes and shrank five

inches, her head barely reaching Beau's chin. "Lead the way."

They ducked into the stairwell. The rubber soles of Beau's running shoes squelched against the steps while her bare feet made her his silent companion.

"We have to go through the lobby to get to the parking garage." She pointed at the metal door on the ground floor.

"Keep your head down." He pushed open the door.

People crisscrossed the lobby on their way back from their business meetings or sightseeing for the day. Deb's gaze darted from group to group, seeing some imagined threat in each one.

Beau hustled her out the side door onto a cement path that led to the garage. He blocked her body with his, his blue eyes wary and alert, his hand nestled in his pocket—the pocket where his gun resided.

He still had her weapon, too. He may be planning to help her rescue Bobby, but he didn't quite trust her.

Should she trust him?

Maybe his willingness to help her was a ploy to get her back to Prospero. And the kiss had been designed to soften her up.

If Beau planned to turn her over to Prospero, he'd learn soon enough she still had a few tricks up her sleeve. She'd fight like a caged animal to save Bobby, even if that meant doing battle against Bobby's father.

She'd put her shoes back on before they hit the lobby and now the clicking sound of the heels echoed on the parking garage's cement floor. "The car's in the next aisle."

She unlocked the car as they approached it. Beau slid into the passenger seat and she tossed the bag into the backseat. Revving the engine, she turned toward him. "Where to?"

He rattled off some directions when they exited the parking structure.

"I wanted to get more info from you before that sniper took aim at your head. Where were you when Bobby was kidnapped? Where do you live?"

"In Virginia, outside of D.C."

"Zendaris sent you to Boston after the kidnapping?"

"Yes. Turn here?"

He nodded. "Is the jewelry heist the first thing he asked of you?"

"After he told me to fly into Logan Airport."

"Do you think Bobby's still in the Virginia area, or do you think he's here?"

"My gut tells me he's here. If the plans are in Boston Zendaris would want to do the swap here, not go back to Virginia." She gripped the steering wheel to stem the tide of panic that washed through her every time she thought about Bobby being held captive by that maniac.

"Any idea what's in Boston?"

"Besides a jewelry store on Beacon Hill? I have no idea. As far as we know, Zendaris doesn't have any connections here."

"Interesting." Beau tapped his chin with his middle finger.

"What's interesting? Boston?"

"The old Deb Sinclair would know that there's a symposium on weapons of the future at MIT this week."

"Really?" Her head jerked his way. She didn't have the heart to tell him the old Deb Sinclair had melted into a puddle on the floor of her son's daycare the day he went missing.

But this new Deb Sinclair wasn't so unfamiliar. This Deb Sinclair, ruled by fear and anger, had controlled the first sixteen years of her life, until she'd had the good fortune to try to steal from Robert Elder.

"I don't think it's a coincidence that Zendaris sent you to Boston at the same time as this gathering. He wants those anti-drone plans. Maybe he thinks one of the symposium's attendees has them."

"This is an international gathering?"

"It is. Scientists and engineers from all over the world will be there."

She drummed her thumbs against the steering wheel, feeling a spark of life for the first time since Bobby's abduction. Her brain clicked and whirred as if coming to life after a long winter hibernation.

"He could be right. Maybe the woman who stole the plans from Stark sold them to the highest bidder before she died. Maybe she had no intention of giving them back to Zendaris."

"The woman who stole the plans is dead? Did Zendaris kill her?"

"One of ours did, self-defense. She was mentally unbalanced."

"Those are the hardest ones to figure out. There's no telling what she did with the plans or why she did it."

"Still, you're right. My presence in Boston at the same time as the symposium is no coincidence. Have the meetings started yet?"

"Meetings have been ongoing for two days."

"Did you connect my being in Boston with this conference?"

"Not until you told me about the anti-drone plans."

"Then why was this symposium even on your radar?"

He turned his head to look out the window. "It's my business to know."

And just like that, Beau the helpful spy morphed into Loki, man of mystery and danger.

She pulled into the loading zone of the new hotel and Beau got them a room.

He dropped onto the passenger seat and tipped his head toward the windshield. "You can park up that ramp."

Ten minutes later they were traipsing down another hotel hallway, but Deb felt less trepidation now that she had Beau by her side. Or should she be feeling more?

His concern could all be an elaborate ruse to lull her into compliance. When she least expected it, her Prospero teammates could crash the party and drag her back for questioning all at Beau's invitation. But her brothers on Team Three had to know she'd never betray them.

Then why not confide in them? The words floated through her mind, and even her answer to that question felt like a betrayal.

Beau pushed open the hotel room door. "One room but two double beds. Hope that's okay."

"That's fine." She tossed the purse onto the bed farthest from the window. "And I hope it's okay that I snag the bed away from the window."

"I was going to suggest it." He clicked the remote control for the TV and swiped a room service menu from the table. "Are you hungry? Maybe we should just eat in the room tonight."

She twitched aside the curtain at the window. "You're sure we weren't followed?"

"Positive." He waved the menu. "Food?"

"Yeah, whatever." She hadn't eaten a decent meal since Zendaris had snatched Bobby.

She plucked the special phone from her pocket and placed it on the nightstand.

Beau said, "He's sure taking his sweet time."

"He's holding all the cards." Deb shrugged out of the coat and hung it in the closet. Then she toed off the heels and stretched out on the bed, stacking a few pillows behind her back and crossing her legs at the ankles.

"I'll order for both of us if that's okay." He peered at her over the top of the menu. "You look like you could use a good meal."

"Food has been low on my list of priorities lately."

"You should know from training that you need to keep yourself in fighting condition."

"You don't get it." That's why she never confided in her Prospero brothers, either. They weren't mothers. When Zendaris had kidnapped her son, he'd carved a hole in her heart. He'd left her half a person.

Beau was Bobby's father, but he didn't know he was a father. He could talk about being in fighting condition and being aware of one's surroundings, but he was a whole person, not a shell like she'd become.

Beau shrugged and picked up the phone. He cradled the receiver against his shoulder as he read off enough dishes to feed the entire hotel.

Deb fluffed up the pillows behind her and stared at the local TV news through half-closed eyes. A shot of MIT had her leaning forward. She snapped her fingers at Beau, who was adding desserts to their order.

She simulated pressing buttons on a remote and he tossed it to her. She increased the volume on the TV.

The voice-over of the reporter droned on about a weapons symposium. The brief report didn't mention any names until the very end.

"Dr. Scott Herndon, professor emeritus at MIT and frequent advisor to the Pentagon, is chairing the symposium, which will include a gala event on the last night to raise funds for war-torn areas across the globe."

When the report ended, Deb muted the sound. "That's it, isn't it? Sounds like a big deal."

"Anything discussed in those meetings is going to be top secret. How does Zendaris expect to get any information out of that symposium?"

"The symposium ends tomorrow." She glanced at the cell phone on the nightstand. "If Zendaris wants me to make a move, you'd think he would've contacted me by now—unless that scope to the forehead was his way of reaching out."

"I don't think Zendaris is trying to kill you. It doesn't add up." Beau perched on the edge of the other bed and rested his ankle on his knee. "Any assignment he has for you will most likely come at the last minute to give you less time to prepare. He wants to keep you off balance."

"He's doing a great job." She tossed the remote to Beau's bed and collapsed against her pillows. "He still hasn't allowed me any contact with Bobby. I don't even know for sure if he's alive or…"

"What's the matter with you?" Beau smacked his hand against his thigh. "You need that proof of life, Deb. Don't do another thing he tells you to do unless you get something on Bobby."

"I demanded it the last time we spoke, but he refused." Crossing her arms, she hunched her shoulders against the persistent chill in her bones.

"You hold some cards here, too. Before you carry out your next assignment, you need assurance of Bobby's safety."

"What if he refuses again and threatens to hurt him? I can't play chicken with my son's life." She rubbed her tingling nose. "What makes this even worse is that Bobby wasn't in the best of health prior to the kidnapping."

"He was sick?"

"He'd been listless, which was so unlike him. I thought he may have caught a bug, but he didn't have any cold or flu symptoms."

"Did you take him to the doctor?"

She slid a glance at Beau, who'd twisted around on the foot of the bed to face her. Did he sense his connection to Bobby on some level?

"He had a doctor's appointment the day before he was snatched. The doc ran some tests on him, took his blood and urine, that type of thing. I haven't heard anything back from the tests yet, but it's only been a week."

"Then you really need to demand to see him or talk to him. What story is Zendaris feeding him?"

"I have no idea. He's only two. I'm sure he doesn't understand why I've abandoned him." She covered her face with her hands. "Once a child is abandoned, he never gets over it."

The mattress sank and Beau encircled her wrists with his fingers. "Nonsense. You recovered nicely. Hell, you're one of the most well-adjusted people I know."

"You don't know me. We spent one night together."

"That's all I need to figure someone out."

She spread her fingers and peeked at him

through the spaces. "That's not saying much considering the types of people you hang out with."

He raised his brows. "When I'm not doing the spy thing, I have the most boring existence you can imagine. My dad's a mechanic, my mom's a secretary at the local high school. Staid. Boring."

"Is that why you went all out on the career path to become one of the most feared assassins in the business?"

His jaw tightened as he shook his head. "I'm no assassin, Deb. Nobody got killed who didn't deserve it. Nobody who wasn't a threat to other lives."

Someone rapped on the door with a shout. "Room service."

Holding out his hand, Beau rose from the bed and crept to the door, lifting his weapon from its holster on the way. He stood to the side of the door and put his eye to the peephole. "Can you slide the check under the door, man? I'll sign it, send it back and you can leave the food."

"Sure."

A slip of paper sailed beneath the door and Beau plucked it from the carpet. He backed up to the credenza and signed the bill. Then he shoved it back through the door and watched from the peephole.

The waiter called out, "Thanks."

Beau waited several seconds and then opened the door and wheeled the cart into the room. "Can't be too careful, huh?"

"If he's been working in hotels a while, I'm sure he's seen everything."

Beau stationed the cart by the table and began lifting silver domes. "Looks good. You hungry?"

The steam that rose from the dishes carried some savory scents that made her mouth water. It had been several days since she'd eaten a real meal, and her stomach grumbled with the realization.

"I *am* hungry."

Beau transferred the plates from the cart to the table and pulled out a chair. "Have a seat."

Deb shook out a thick white napkin and dropped it on her lap. She started with the soup and didn't stop until she'd licked the last smudge of cream cheese frosting from her fork.

"How long has it been since you've eaten more than a few bites of food?"

She patted her mouth with the napkin. "Since the day they took Bobby."

"I thought so. You look—" his gaze dipped from her face to her body and back again "—a little thinner than when I last saw you."

Warmth crept into her cheeks and she covered the bottom half of her face with the napkin, pretending to wipe her mouth again. He should know.

They'd spent almost the entire night naked in her hotel room. They'd eaten room service that night, too, but not seated at a table with napkins in their laps. They'd lounged across the king-size bed, feeding each other morsels of food, even incorporating the chocolate cake into their love-making. Instead of daintily patting their mouths with napkins, they'd hauled off to the shower, together.

She coughed. "Being a mom keeps me on my toes. I don't have as much time to work out at the gym, but I get to run at the playground and throw balls and chase after a speeding tricycle."

"Sounds like you love it...and him."

Deb studied his face. Was it time to tell him Bobby was his? *Nope.* Loki wouldn't want to be saddled with a son anyway. How could he squeeze in a battle with Somali pirates between Little League games?

Beau Slater may have come from ordinary, but he didn't want to go back there.

The cell phone by the bed chirped. The fork she'd been dragging across a plate dropped with a clatter and she half rose from her chair.

"It's him."

"Answer it. It's what you've been waiting for."

She swallowed and all the sweetness from the carrot cake dissolved like ashes on her tongue.

When the phone rang for the fourth time, she dived across the bed and grabbed it.

"Yes?"

"Good job at the jewelry store. You can keep the loot."

"I don't want it. What was the point of that? Someone could've gotten hurt."

Beau jerked his thumb up, and she punched a button for the speaker.

"Someone would've gotten hurt if you hadn't followed our instructions, Deb. Just look at it that way."

"I—I'm in a different hotel. Someone was aiming a high-powered weapon into my hotel room this afternoon. I saw the beam on the wall."

Zendaris sucked in a breath. "Are you scamming me, Deb?"

"Are you scamming me? Are you trying to kill me?"

"Why would I do that? We're just getting started." He clicked his tongue. "But maybe your colleagues want you dead."

"Never." Her gaze darted toward Beau slumped in his chair, his fingers steepled beneath his chin. Why had Prospero sent the best in the business after her?

"Are you sure about that? If the mighty Jack Coburn gets wind of your betrayal, you're finished."

She ground her teeth together. "It's not a betrayal if it's coerced."

"But they don't know that, do they? Do they, Deb?"

"As far as Prospero is concerned, I'm on a leave of absence. They have no reason to suspect otherwise."

"Where are you?"

"Another hotel in Cambridge." She held her breath. Would he demand the location?

"Excellent."

"What next, Zendaris? A bank robbery? A high-speed chase?"

"A party."

She raised her shoulders at Beau. "You want me to go to a party?"

"A very special party with very special people."

"Where?" Deb licked her lips.

"In Boston. You'll be attending the gala fundraiser as part of the Symposium on Alternate Methods of Defense."

"What do you want me to do at this party besides eat, drink and be merry?"

"I want you to get close to Dr. Scott Herndon."

"Get close to him and do what?"

"Kill him."

Chapter Five

Beau bolted upright. The man couldn't be serious.

Deb choked out one word. "Why?"

"That's not your concern for now. Let's just say I'm sending a message."

"How am I supposed to kill Dr. Herndon in a roomful of people?" She shook her head at Beau, her eyes wide and glassy.

He wanted to go to her and smooth away the worry, but now wasn't the time. And what could he possibly say to comfort her? The man had her son and she'd do anything to protect him.

"I'm leaving the logistics of the crime in your capable Prospero hands, Deb. You figure it out, but at the end of the evening Dr. Herndon will no longer be drawing breath."

Beau vaulted from the chair and tapped Deb on the knee. He mouthed, *Bobby.*

She closed her eyes. "I'm not killing Dr. Herndon or anyone else until I have proof that my son is okay."

"He's fine, just a little tired. You'll see when I decide you'll see."

Beau squeezed her knee and shook his head. Zendaris needed her. She had the power right now.

"No. I need to see or talk to him before the event tomorrow night, or it's not happening."

Zendaris paused and then sighed. "All right. Not tonight. Tomorrow morning. Are you ready for your instructions?"

For the next five minutes, Zendaris explained to Deb how to pick up her ticket to the event, her identity for the evening, and the dress code. He must've given her that wad of cash in the bag to carry out her assignments without leaving a trail of credit card receipts.

When she ended the call, Beau held out his hand for the phone and she dropped it in his palm.

He examined it again, but couldn't see any way to track the number or location of the phone Zendaris used to call her. He didn't want to take the device apart in case that sent some sort of signal to Zendaris.

"I can't kill someone."

"You're not going to kill Dr. Herndon. We'll figure out a way to trick Zendaris."

"I don't see how. The death of Dr. Scott Herndon is going to be big news."

"Prospero never faked a death before?"

"Prospero may have but I haven't."

"I have, so you're in luck."

She crossed her legs beneath her and pushed the hair from her face. "You were right about demanding to see Bobby. He gave in."

"Of course he did." He dropped the phone back on the bed. "Zendaris needs you. If he harms Bobby now, you're no longer his puppet."

"You were also right about that defense symposium."

"It would've been clear to you, too, Deb, if you'd been thinking straight. That's half of Zendaris's advantage over you, and he knows it. You're rattled. But he didn't count on me."

"I never thought I could count on you, either." She grabbed his arm. "Why are you really helping me, Beau? Are you hoping to bag Zendaris on your own? I can't believe you'd put my son before that goal."

"Why do you keep asking me that question, Deb? I told you the prospect of getting close to Zendaris is tempting, but I'm not going to put a child's life at risk to do it." He traced the knuckles of her hand. "Can you put aside your trust issues for a while to believe me?"

She released his arm, leaving crescent imprints

from her fingernails. "I don't know why I should trust you. I never figured you for a family man with any strong feelings for children. So it makes me wonder even more why you're torpedoing your own assignment to help me."

"Maybe I don't have strong feelings for children." He ran a hand along her thigh. "But that doesn't mean I don't have some feelings for you."

"Do you always run around jeopardizing your career for one-night stands?"

"Are you done eating?" He pushed off the bed and began loading plates and serving dishes back onto the cart.

"I'm glad I ate before that phone call because I just lost my appetite." She rolled onto her stomach and planted her elbows on the bed while balancing her chin in one palm. "What did you think of Zendaris?"

He clanged a silver cover back over a serving dish. "A scumbag of the highest order."

"I mean, do you think that was him on the phone? Have you ever heard his voice?"

"No." He dabbed at a cake crumb and sucked it into his mouth. "I know he's of Greek descent and spent time in Italy, so the accent of the guy on the phone would match that. I thought Prospero finally got a line on him. That was the chatter."

"We did. The former nanny for Zendaris's children was able to give us a composite. We know what he looks like now—when he's not in disguise."

"But he's always in disguise."

"Just like you."

"Not always." He ran a hand through his hair, shorter than he usually wore it. "This is my real hair, my real eye color."

"You've been known to sport a beard, long hair, glasses, extra weight. Why no disguise for this assignment?"

He shoved the cart ahead of him toward the door. "I guess I wanted you to recognize me. I didn't wear a disguise that night, either."

"You didn't wear much of anything that night."

"Glad you noticed." He gripped the handles of the cart to the breaking point and wheeled it to the door.

Her low, throaty voice and half-lidded eyes had caused a jolt of lust to claim half his body—the bottom half. This was the Deb he remembered. This was the Deb he still wanted.

But she'd pushed him away after the kiss. Why the mixed messages now? Her emotions were all over the place. The fear she felt for her son caused her to seek solace, and maybe the only way she knew how to elicit comfort from him was through seduction. Maybe she just wanted some physical contact, but the only physical contact they knew was sexual.

Probably wasn't a good idea to mix business with pleasure, so much pleasure. But then it hadn't been a good idea to take this assignment in the first place. He should've come clean to Prospero about his heated fling with Deb.

He shoved the cart against the wall in the hallway and stepped back into the room. "You have a long day ahead of you tomorrow. You should get some rest. Do you have toiletries? Do you want me to pick some up downstairs? I at least need a toothbrush."

"That would be great. I flew into Logan this morning. Zendaris didn't tell me to pack a bag, so I didn't."

"I'll pick up the basics, and you can get more of what you need tomorrow when you go shopping for the party dress."

"Do you think he's watching me?"

"He seemed genuinely surprised by the sniper, and he didn't ask you the details of your hotel. I don't think so. He doesn't need to. He has his insurance.

"Keep the door locked and chained and don't open it for anyone." He strode to the window and pulled the drapes closed even though their window faced the Charles River. "And stay away from the window."

He slipped out the door and paused with his

head bent until he heard the lock and chain slide into place.

Waiting for the elevator, he glanced to his left when he heard a door close. He poked his head into the corridor, but all the doors remained closed. Maybe someone had gone for ice or the vending machine.

He rolled his shoulders and stabbed at the elevator button again. He was on edge and it felt good, natural. He'd let his encounter with Deb throw him off his stride. His assignment may have changed but he was still on assignment. Still on the job.

The elevator skimmed down to the first floor without stopping. He crossed the lobby and headed for the shop he'd seen when he'd checked in.

He bought some toothpaste, toothbrushes, a comb and several other items to get them through the night and the next morning. As he grabbed the small bag with his purchases, his cell phone buzzed once in his pocket.

He exited the store and leaned against the wall outside the restaurant bar. He checked the phone's display and sucked in a breath. *Prospero.*

If he ignored the message, he wouldn't have to lie to Jack. If he ignored the message, Jack would read that as totally out of character for Loki.

If Jack wanted status, he'd give Jack status.

He'd tell him he'd tracked the quarry to Boston—not a lie. Prospero wouldn't send anyone else out here to check on his progress. The stalwart men of Prospero trusted him.

That was their first mistake.

He sent a text that he might have a lead on Deb heading to Boston. The only response he got from Jack was *Roger*.

Yeah, the man still trusted him. But Beau had no intention of letting Jack down, or letting Deb down. He'd stay true to Prospero, help Deb and rescue her son as icing on the cake.

When he got back to the room, he tapped on the door and stood in full view of the peephole. The hotel staff had removed the room service cart.

The chain scraped in its slot and the door inched open. Beau pushed it wide. "Are you okay?"

Deb rubbed her eyes. "I fell asleep. What took you so long?" She yawned and held out her hand for the bag swinging from his fingertips.

She didn't need to know he'd had contact with Jack. He tossed the bag to her. "I had a lot of shopping to do."

Peering into the bag, she wrinkled her nose. "I'm going to have to do a lot better than this when I hit that party tomorrow night."

"You and me both."

Her eyes widened as she looked up. "You're going, too?"

"How else are we going to stage a murder?"

DEB ROLLED ONTO her stomach and burrowed her head into the pillow, trying to cling to the fading wisps of her dream. Its images had already slipped from her consciousness, but the dream had left her with a feeling of contentment—a feeling all too rare in the daylight hours.

She hadn't slept that peacefully since the day she'd lost Bobby, and she owed that sound sleep to the man in the next bed.

Shifting her head on the pillow, she opened one eye and drank in the sight of Beau sprawled on the bed next to hers, one bare leg hanging off the side, both arms wrapped around a pillow.

He stirred and murmured something into the pillow.

Was he having sweet dreams, too? She'd wanted nothing more than to crawl under the covers with him last night, but she recognized the urge for what it was—a need for comfort. He was already doing his part. She couldn't ask him for his shoulder to lean on in addition to everything else he was doing for her.

He didn't owe her anything. Hell, he didn't even know Bobby was his son.

She cleared her throat and the noise acted like a prod.

Beau's eyes flew open and he bolted upright in the bed. "What?"

"I'm sorry. I just coughed. I didn't mean to wake you up." In fact, she'd been enjoying studying his face in repose. Now she was enjoying the way the sheet had fallen to his waist, exposing his bare chest.

Maybe she did want more than comfort from Beau. The fire she'd felt when she'd first met him had never died. Being with him again had ignited the kindling flame.

She averted her gaze. Her attraction for Beau caused knots of guilt to form in her belly. Zendaris had her son. How could she even be thinking about sex?

Did that make her a bad mother? The fact that she'd allowed her son to be kidnapped made her a bad mother. Cade Stark would've never allowed that to happen to his son.

She buried her face in the pillow.

"Do you want to have breakfast downstairs before we go shopping?"

"Zendaris is supposed to send me confirmation that Bobby is okay today, before the party."

Beau swung his legs over the side of the bed and planted his feet on the floor with the sheet still twisted around his torso. "He'll use that cell phone to do it. Keep it with you."

"The only clothes I have are the ones I wore yesterday." She scooted up against the headboard. "I brought some cash with me, so I'm going to pick up a pair of jeans and a few shirts."

"All I have is yesterday's clothes, too. I'm going to need a tux for tonight."

"You still haven't explained how you're going to get into that party."

"One of the guests is going to lose his ticket. Isn't that what Zendaris told you? All guests needed a ticket?"

"He said he'd leave mine for me today."

"Obviously, if he has you go to a pickup location, you go alone. He and his cohorts might be watching." Beau rose from the bed and the covers fell from his body.

His boxer briefs clung to his heavily muscled thighs, and he stretched, the rest of his muscles shifting and bunching.

"And tonight?" Deb swallowed and tugged the sheet up to her chin. "We'll have to go separately tonight."

"Yeah, just in case he's watching the crowd. I doubt it though. He's not going to want to be anywhere near that party especially since Prospero now has an accurate description of him."

"But he's the master of disguise."

Beau shrugged. "Aren't we all? Do you want the shower first?"

"Go ahead."

When Beau disappeared into the bathroom, Deb turned up the volume on the TV. She didn't need to hear the water running and imagine how Beau looked with it sluicing across the planes of his body. She didn't have to imagine because she'd seen it—and him—in the flesh.

Amazing how that one night of unbridled passion had led to Bobby, and in a twisted way had led them back to each other. She'd figured Bobby's paternity had been her ace in the hole to sway Beau from hunting her to helping her. And she hadn't even needed it to convince him.

He'd been ready to help her as soon as she'd explained her predicament to him. He hadn't needed to hear that Bobby was his.

The shower stream stopped and several minutes later, Beau called from the bathroom. "It's all yours, and I even left you some hot water."

They hadn't had that problem when they'd showered together.

She dragged the sheet from the bed and wrapped it around her body. She shuffled toward the bathroom, clutching her wrinkled skirt and blouse under one arm.

Holding her breath, she squeezed past Beau standing at the vanity mirror, the white hotel towel wrapped around his waist, heat emanating from his body.

"I won't be long."

"Where's the phone in case he contacts you while you're in the shower?"

She opened her hand. "I have it."

"Leave it here." He tapped the vanity.

She scooted around him to place the phone on the countertop. Then she dove into the bathroom and shut the door. Releasing a sigh, she dropped the sheet and shimmied out of her underwear.

He hadn't lied. The hot water pounded her back and she closed her eyes.

If they could somehow fool Zendaris into believing that she killed Dr. Herndon, would she get Bobby back? She believed Beau when he'd told her that he'd accomplished similar feats in his storied career. She'd known the career before she'd met the man, and he hadn't disappointed her at all. In any way.

The pounding on the bathroom door jolted her out of her reverie.

"Deb, you have a text."

She cranked off the faucet and yanked her towel from the rack. "Give me a minute."

She squeezed out her hair and tucked the towel around her body. Still dripping, she threw open the door to the vanity. "Did you open it?"

"No." He held the phone out to her and she took it with a damp hand.

It took her two tries to hit the right button to open the text message. The picture that greeted her had her sinking to the floor in a puddle.

"What is it?" Beau hovered above her. "Are you okay?"

She turned the phone out toward him, tears flooding her eyes. "It's Bobby."

Chapter Six

He crouched beside her, his bare shoulder touching hers. He poked at the display. "Can you blow that up? He's holding a newspaper."

She flicked the pads of her finger across the display and the picture of Bobby enlarged.

"More." Beau closed his hand over hers and brought the phone closer to his face. He peered at the screen. "It's a newspaper from today. Proof of life."

Pressing the phone against her heart, she breathed out, "Thank God."

"How does he look to you?"

She held the phone out again and refocused the picture. "He looks sleepy. He must've just woken up. How does he look to you?"

Beau squinted at his son's face. Would he see the resemblance? "He looks tired."

"I'm so worried he might be sick. How would they know? How would they know what he needed?"

He stood up, one hand on her head, tousling

her wet locks. "One thing at a time. Let's just get him back."

Deb dressed and dried her hair before the mirror using the hotel hair dryer. Zendaris wanted her in disguise again tonight but not with the blond wig. After all, that woman had just robbed a jewelry store.

She hunched over the vanity practically touching her nose to the mirror. And this one would be an assassin.

Zendaris had given her plenty of money to effect her change of identity, and now that he'd given her proof of Bobby's safety he'd expect her to carry out his orders. Or else.

She shivered and backed away from the mirror. "I'm ready."

Beau, wearing the same jeans and blue flannel shirt from yesterday, shrugged off the wall where he'd been leaning and pocketed his phone.

Deb stumbled to a stop. "Who were you calling?"

"Just checking my messages." He patted the phone in his pocket.

"Anyone I know?" She held her breath, her gaze scanning his impassive face. Did she really expect Loki to give away anything with his expression? In his line of work, losing your poker face could get you killed.

"A new contract coming up." He raised his

brows. "Do you think I'd come this far with you to double-cross you?"

"I don't know." She strode to the closet and yanked her coat from the hanger. "Just remember…"

He sliced a hand through the air. "You don't have to tell me. You won't go without a fight."

She shot him a thumbs-up. "You're catching on."

"Let's eat."

She draped her coat over her arm as he ushered her through the door. She'd misjudged him. She never dreamed he'd ride to her rescue if he didn't have a stake in the outcome. Maybe he knew subconsciously that Bobby was his but was too afraid to ask. The timing was right, although she'd fudged a little and had told him Bobby was almost two when he was really over two years old.

As they waited for the elevator, she whispered, "Do you have your weapon?"

"Of course."

She knew he had it but wanted to segue into her next question. "When am I getting mine back?"

"Just as soon as I can be sure you're not going to use it against me and go rogue."

"Why would I do that? I'm grateful for your help. I don't think I could do this without you."

He snorted. "Deb Sinclair, first female Prospero agent? That'll be the day she's helpless."

"I told you." She jabbed at the button a few more times. "I'm different from the woman you met that night."

"Not so different." His gaze raked her head to toe.

The doors opening and the people inside the car saved her from a response. They had to dissipate this sexual tension between them. It wouldn't help her cause. It wouldn't save Bobby.

Maybe they should just sleep together and get it over with. They'd probably come away from the encounter disappointed that it didn't live up to the fireworks of their one and only night as a couple.

Beau placed his fingers on her hip when the elevator reached the lobby, and Deb squirmed at his touch. She knew in her heart this man could never disappoint her.

They nabbed a table in the lobby restaurant and ordered breakfast. Beau pulled a smartphone from his pocket, not the same phone he'd been checking when she'd walked in on him. Looks as if everyone had special phones.

He tapped the display several times. "I need to rent a tux for tonight and pick up a few things for my transformation."

"Do you think we should be seen together on

the street?" Deb poured a steady stream of cream in her black coffee.

"I don't think Zendaris is following you. He doesn't even know what hotel you're staying in anymore, and doesn't seem to care. But it's not a bad idea for us to keep our distance on the street." He tilted the phone back and forth. "If you pick up a throwaway cell phone, I'll text you to let you know where I'll be, and you can do the same. Doesn't mean we can't wind up at the same shops, but let's not arrive and leave together."

Using a napkin, he jotted down the addresses of places that would be of interest to her and shoved it across the table. "Let me know when Zendaris contacts you to pick up your ticket to the ball. I want to scope out the place."

"I'm going to feel a little like Cinderella." She folded the napkin and dropped it into the bag hanging on the back of her chair.

He quirked one eyebrow. "I think I missed that part of the story where Cinderella had to take someone out."

Deb took the T into Boston and her first stop was an upscale wig store. She felt naked without Beau by her side and felt even more naked without her weapon. He should've trusted her with it.

Zendaris hadn't given her instructions about her appearance—just that she be appropriately dressed for the gala and not look anything like the jewelry store thief.

She fingered the hair of the wigs lined up on mannequin heads with blank faces. She stared into the vacant eyes of one face and felt as if she were looking into a mirror.

She'd felt empty, drained since Bobby's kidnapping.

"Can I help you?" The clerk glided forward on the thick carpet.

"I'm looking for something—" Deb cranked her head back and forth "—black. Long, straight and black."

The woman cocked her head. "That would be a very dramatic look with your pale coloring." Crooking her finger, she crossed to the other side of the store. "I think I have what you want."

Only Zendaris had what she wanted now.

The saleswoman slipped a wig off the smooth dome of one of the mannequins and held it up. "Is this what you're looking for?"

The long black locks brushed the woman's arm as it swayed in her hand.

"Perfect."

"Have a seat." The clerk patted a chair stationed before a mirror.

Deb perched in the chair while the woman gathered her hair in a ponytail, pinned it up and pulled a cap over her head. She tucked in the stray auburn strands and pulled the wig over the cap.

When Deb looked up, she saw a stranger. The silky black strands cascaded across her shoulders and down her back. Now she just needed some dark eyes.

Her next stop was a department store cosmetics counter. She couldn't bring herself to buy a bunch of expensive cosmetics, so she asked for some samples and figured she'd pick up the rest at the drugstore. Then she took a detour through the store to pick up a few items of clothing so she wouldn't be stuck wearing the same skirt and blouse for however long Zendaris planned to keep her on the hook.

She hoped to God it wasn't much longer. Bobby looked too sleepy in that picture even for morning. Did they keep him tied up? Was he imprisoned in some room? A wave of nausea hit her gut, and she doubled over the clothes rack. She had to rescue her little boy.

She scooped in a couple of breaths, inhaling the floral perfume she'd sprayed on her wrists at the makeup counter. She could do this. She could get through this. She had no choice.

She swung by the lingerie department and snapped up several pairs of panties and grabbed a pair of pajamas on the sale table. If she had to spend another night in a hotel room with Beau, she preferred to do so with a few extra layers of clothing.

The shopping bags hung from her arms and banged against her thighs as she hailed a taxi to take her to her last stop—time to find the perfect dress for a murder.

She slipped into the formal wear shop slightly out of breath. What she saw next sucked the rest of the breath from her lungs.

Beau was planted in front of a mirror, tugging on the cuffs of a black dinner jacket. His eyes met hers briefly in the glass. "You don't think the sleeves are a little short?"

The saleswoman fluttered around him like a butterfly. "Maybe a little. It's the shoulders that concern me. Yours are so broad the material is puckering across your back."

Deb pursed her lips in a smirk. Could the woman be more obvious? She cleared her throat.

The woman responded without taking her eyes from Beau. "Someone will be right with you."

That someone was another clerk who popped her head out of the dressing room area. "Have a look around. I'll be there in a minute."

Deb cut a wide swath around Beau and the fawning store clerk. She cruised the perimeter of the store, fingering fabrics and checking price tags—not that any of the dollar signs concerned her. Zendaris was picking up the tab.

A couple thousand bucks for a dress in exchange for an assassination? Her services came cheap.

The clerk from the back approached her, brushing her hands together. "With your coloring, I'm thinking a jewel-toned green. What's the occasion?"

Deb didn't have the heart to tell the girl that by the time the evening rolled around, her coloring would be completely different. "It's a formal event—gowns, tuxes."

"Ooh, the best kind. Can I show you some dark emerald-greens over here?"

Deb clung to the black dress in her hands. You couldn't wear green to a murder, could you? "I was thinking something a little more subtle. I sort of want to blend in with the crowd."

The clerk screwed up her mouth. "That's no fun, but black is definitely your color for blending in."

After several minutes of frantic activity, the girl sent Deb to the dressing room where she'd stashed three black dresses—a halter neckline, strapless and spaghetti straps.

She stepped into the halter dress first and let it drop as soon as she brought the ties around her neck—too severe. She shimmied into the strapless dress and tugged at the fitted bodice. Nice.

The clerk called from outside the dressing room door. "Do you want a second opinion?"

Hiking up the dress, Deb stepped out of the dressing room and twirled around. "What do you think?"

"It's amazing."

Deb jerked her head around at the sound of Beau's voice. Back in his jeans, he sprawled in a chair across from the dressing rooms, a bottle of sparkling water in one hand.

The clerk giggled.

"Excuse me?"

"The dress, take it. It's you."

She added a note of outrage to her voice. "I don't believe I asked your opinion."

"I just couldn't help noticing how great it looks on you."

"Mr. Shelton." The saleswoman who had been helping Beau stepped between them with a plastic bag draped over her arm. "Your tux is ready."

Beau eased to his feet. "Thanks, Adele." He strolled to the door and called over his shoulder, "Maybe we'll wind up at the same black-tie event."

He'd *better* be there.

Deb bought the strapless black dress and a pair of heels to go with it. Then she loaded her purchases in a taxi and returned to the hotel.

On the way to the elevator, she glanced at

the big clock over the reception desk—past two o'clock and still no word from Zendaris on where to pick up her ticket for tonight's party. Would Beau really be able to find a way to attend?

The bigger question was how did he plan to fake an assassination at a crowded event?

By the time she reached the room, her arms were aching from the weight of her bags. She tapped at the door with the toe of her shoe.

Beau opened the door, and she transferred two bags from her hands to his.

Hoisting the bags, he asked, "What is all this stuff?"

"Since I didn't get to pack before I left home, I wanted to pick up a few things to wear when I'm not attending gala fundraisers." She collapsed on the bed, her legs hanging over the side. "Did you get everything you needed?"

He dug into one of his bags in the corner of the room and bounced what looked like a caterpillar in his hand. "Zendaris isn't the only one who can change appearances."

"What is that thing?"

He held it up between two fingers. "A fake moustache."

"You're really going all out." She kicked off her shoes and wiggled her toes. She couldn't wait to slip into that pair of flats she'd bought today.

"You didn't hear anything from Zendaris?"

"Not yet." She rolled to her stomach. "You don't think he changed his mind, do you?"

"Probably not, but that's a good thing. You want to do whatever is going to get you closer to getting your son back."

"Including murder?" She pulled a pillow against her chest and hugged it. "I don't understand how we're going to get around that."

"We will. Let's have some lunch."

"I'm not hungry." The dinner last night and the breakfast this morning had been more food than she'd eaten in a week. The meals had made her feel slow and sluggish and too relaxed. She needed to be on top of her game right now.

"Didn't your mother ever tell you that food helps you keep up your strength?" Beau cursed, realizing his mistake almost before the words left his mouth. "Sorry."

"Yeah, I never had that mother, but I know what you mean."

"I worked up an appetite with all that shopping." He peeled his key card from the glass-topped credenza. "I'm going to run to that deli down the street and pick up a sandwich. Don't go anywhere without me, and keep the door locked and chained."

He backed out of the room, shoving the key card in his back pocket. *What an idiot.* He knew Deb hadn't had a mother growing up. Her mother had been some junkie who'd abandoned her to the foster care system at the age of four.

Deb hadn't even had the advantage of being a baby ready for adoption. The older kids always had a tougher time of it, and she'd bounced around a few foster families before running away from the last one at sixteen.

The rigors and discipline of the U.S. Navy must've been a welcome change from the chaos of her childhood. And then she'd learned to fly choppers.

He jogged down the stairs and welcomed the brisk blast of air that hit his face when he bounded outside. Between all the hot and heavy lovemaking he and Deb had indulged in, it was amazing he'd learned so much about her life.

Shoving his hands in his pockets, he kept his head down as he strode to the deli. He'd feel a lot better once he donned his wig and facial hair. With that symposium in town, he risked running into people who knew him.

He'd missed the lunch rush and stood in line behind just one other customer. While he waited for his pastrami, his phone buzzed. Deb's name flashed on his display.

"What's up?"

"It's on."

"Where?"

"I have instructions to pick up the ticket at a bookstore on White Street, Flights of Fancy."

"A bookstore?"

"In a book. The ticket's going to be in a book."

"Hold on." Beau put down the phone and paid for the sandwich. "What time?"

"In an hour."

Pulling up his sleeve, he glanced at his watch. "I'm going to head over there right now, Deb. Zendaris is not going to risk leaving that ticket in a book for long. Maybe someone's slipping it into the book as we speak."

"Are you going to do anything if you catch someone?"

"No. We want that ticket, but I might be able to get a line on someone working with Zendaris. Give me the address and the name of the book."

Deb gave him the information. He could probably walk to the bookstore, but a taxi would get him there faster. He headed back to the hotel to pick one up there.

A five-minute taxi ride brought him to the bookstore, and he instructed the driver to drop him off another hundred feet down the street.

Shoving his hands in his pockets and tucking his chin to his chest, he jogged across the street and dropped his sandwich on one of the metal tables on the patio in front of a coffeehouse. Then he ducked inside to order a coffee and grab a magazine and took a seat at the table.

He shook open the magazine and unwrapped his sandwich. He alternated between taking bites of his pastrami and peering over the top of the magazine to monitor foot traffic into the bookstore.

Each time someone entered or exited the store, he snapped them with his camera. Maybe they'd get lucky. He didn't believe for a minute Zendaris would risk some stranger finding the ticket to the fundraiser by placing it too early. He'd want to know that Deb could get to the bookstore first.

A couple of likely suspects, both male, shuffled into the store and then out again in record time. Beau wouldn't dismiss any women as likely candidates, but the truth was there weren't many Deb Sinclairs in the world.

And for one hot night, she'd belonged to him.

After more surveillance pictures and several unread magazine pages, a taxi pulled up to the curb fronting the bookstore and deposited Deb on the sidewalk, sporting a long black ponytail. A pair of slim jeans and black flats had replaced the straight skirt and high heels of the past few days. Dark sunglasses hid half her face. She looked young and fresh enough to be a student in this town teeming with them.

His pulse quickened at the sight of her.

She glanced both ways and slipped into the store. The minutes ticked by on Beau's watch, each one passing slower than the previous one. He slurped the last of his cold coffee and chucked the magazine onto the table.

Several more minutes passed, and then Deb emerged from the store, her sunglasses on top of her head. She must've asked the taxi to wait because the same one barreled down the street as Deb stepped onto the curb.

Beau scraped his chair back, tossed his coffee cup and sandwich paper into the trash and dropped the magazine back in the rack just inside the coffee place.

He decided to walk back to the hotel, welcoming the cold air that needled his face. Now that Deb had her ticket to tonight's festivities, he had to beg, borrow or steal his own. He had no intention of leaving her in that lion's den by herself.

If Zendaris wanted a murder, he'd get a murder.

He used his key card to enter the room, but Deb had chained the door. Her instincts seemed to be returning to her after the shock of losing her son.

"It's me."

She shut the door and slid the chain. She greeted him holding a laminated rectangle in front of her.

Before studying the ticket, his gaze locked on her eyes, now brown instead of green. Her emerald eyes had given her face a bright, open aspect. This stranger hid secrets behind her dark eyes.

"Nice disguise."

She waved the ticket back and forth. "I thought I might be able to slip outside and give this to you once I was in, but it has a UPN code. Some attendant at the door will most likely scan the ticket so that it can't be used again."

"That UPN makes it hard to duplicate, too." He pinched the plastic between his fingers and turned the ticket over. "Looks like I'm just going to have to steal one."

"Do you think you can do that?"

He rolled his eyes and handed the ticket back to her. "You're the one fond of calling me Loki."

"I didn't realize Loki was a thief along with all his other talents."

"Some of Loki's exploits are exaggerated—" he flicked a finger at the small camera he'd taken from his pocket "—and some aren't."

"Is that a camera?"

"Yes, Madam Spy. I don't leave home without it."

"Do you think you caught Zendaris's associate?"

"Associate? That's a nice name for him." He claimed his laptop from the closet, placed it on the table by the window and booted it up. "Tell me if you recognize any of these people. Maybe the guy who dropped the phone in your pocket on that street corner."

Deb paced the room while he fiddled with the USB connection between his mini camera and the laptop. Soon the images loaded. "They're up."

Deb leaned over him, her black ponytail sliding over her shoulder and tickling his arm. Her scent, a mingling of flowers and musk and citrus, made his head swim. Or maybe it was her close proximity and the way her warm breath caressed his cheek that made him dizzy.

He tapped the keyboard to scroll through each image. "Any of these people look familiar?"

At the third picture, Deb jabbed the screen. "This guy."

Beau zeroed in on his face and blew up the image. The man in the picture also had on sunglasses that hid a portion of his face and a hat pulled low on his forehead. Was everyone in Boston sporting some kind of disguise?

"No." She wiggled her fingers at the screen. "Zoom out again. It's not his face. It's his body. The guy who bumped into me on the street in Beacon Hill had a large build, a puffy jacket like this guy and broad shoulders, a thick neck—or at least his jacket made it seem thick."

Beau hit the arrow key several times until

the man's body filled the frame. "He's big, wide through the torso, neck as big as one of my thighs. Do you think it's the same guy?"

"Could be. Was he one of the first ones you caught at the bookstore?"

"Yep. He's my third suspect. Look through the rest before you settle on him." He clicked through the slideshow for her, and she halted at only one more—another big guy in a leather jacket.

"The first one had the right kind of jacket on. It could be him. His face isn't very distinctive, is it?"

"All heads and faces have distinct shapes and forms. I'm sending this one to my guy to see what comes back."

She stepped back and curled her fingers around the back of his chair. "You have a guy?"

"You have Prospero. I have a support team, too."

"Do they know what you're working on?"

"Never."

She puckered her lips and blew out a long breath. "Haven't you had to check in with Prospero yet? Aren't they demanding some kind of progress report from you?"

"I'm Loki, not a second-grader." He cropped and saved the photo and then sent it along to one of the computer banks that matched faces with a huge database of known and suspected terrorists, thugs and wannabes. "This could take a while, but then we have a party to attend."

"Three hours to go. How are you going to get that ticket?"

"I'm a skilled pickpocket." He flexed and then cracked his knuckles. "You don't think swiping one of these tickets from some distracted scientist isn't going to be child's play for Loki?"

She laughed and some of the lines that had been plaguing her face disappeared. "Not every scientist is forgetful and distracted."

"I'll find one who is." Crossing his arms behind his head, he stretched out his legs. "I had a sandwich for lunch. Do you want to eat something before the party?"

"I can't eat." Deb folded her hands across her stomach. "Too nervous. We still haven't discussed the plan for this evening. How are we going to pull off a fake murder?"

"We'll have to assess the situation first. Maybe I can get close to Dr. Herndon and make a proposal."

"He's not going to listen to some deranged stranger and agree to play possum."

"Who said Dr. Herndon and I are strangers?"

"You know Dr. Herndon?" Her newly dark eyes popped open.

"You could say that."

She huffed out a breath and her nostrils flared. "Why don't you just say it?"

"We all have our secrets, Deb."

Her cheeks flushed and she turned away.

He planned to help her rescue her son, but that didn't mean he had to reveal all his secrets. He shoved the laptop into the middle of the table. "If you don't mind, I'm going to hit the hotel gym before I start my transformation."

"That's fine." She poked her head in the closet to retrieve the small evening clutch she'd bought earlier and stuffed the ticket inside.

Did Beau suspect her of hiding something from him? Every time he mentioned keeping secrets, she felt as if he were drilling a hole into her brain to discover hers.

If he couldn't see the obvious similarity between himself and Bobby, she didn't want to bring it up. This was not the time or place to tell a man he had a son.

"I'm going to get some rest and then start my own transformation. I'm sure mine's going to take longer than yours."

He pointed to his head. "You already got started. You… It looks great, different."

"That's the idea."

He left for the gym and waited outside the door, listening for the chain. She appreciated the protectiveness but she'd feel a lot safer if she had her weapon.

He'd locked both guns in the room safe but had neglected to give her the combination. Did he really think she'd up and shoot him to escape after everything he'd done for her?

He might up and shoot her once she revealed she'd kept his son from him these past two years. He had to understand. She'd make him understand, or maybe she wouldn't have to try. Once he finished this assignment, he'd be traipsing off to his next one.

Maybe not *traipse*. Beau wasn't a man who traipsed.

Sighing, she dropped onto the edge of the bed and slipped off her new flats, and then curled onto her side. She reached for the phone on the nightstand and clicked open the picture of Bobby holding the newspaper.

She traced his sweet face with her fingertip. "Hold on, precious. Mommy's coming. Daddy, too."

Chapter Seven

By the time Beau returned from his workout, Deb had showered, slipped into her lingerie and hugged a white terry-cloth robe around her body to let him into the room.

He tilted his head back and sniffed. "It smells sweet in here—a lot better than that gym."

"It's the perfume. I talked the girl at the cosmetics counter into giving me a few sample sizes of perfume, even though I crossed the street to buy my makeup at the drugstore."

He snorted. "Don't waste your time trying to be thrifty with Zendaris's money."

"Oh, I don't care about that." She pulled a chair up to the mirror. "I just want to be able to dump all this stuff once this mission is over. I don't think I could bring myself to throw out expensive makeup regardless of who footed the bill for it."

She spread a hand towel on the table and started lining up tubes and jars and brushes. "How was your workout?"

"I really needed it." He stripped off his sweaty T-shirt and shoved it into a plastic bag in the closet.

Deb leaned close to the mirror, but shifted her gaze to the reflection behind her. Beau must've done some shopping on his own, too. She hadn't remembered the gym shorts that now hung low on his waist.

When he raised his eyes to meet her stare in the mirror, she snatched at a bottle of foundation, knocking it over. She'd better stop acting like a love-struck teenager around him.

Her focus had to remain on Bobby and freeing him from his captors. Somehow she felt as though, if she stopped thinking about him for one minute, he'd be snatched from her.

She'd been preoccupied the day he'd disappeared. Logically, she knew her preoccupation had nothing to do with Bobby's abduction, but that didn't lessen the guilt. She didn't need any more guilt weighing her down.

"I'm going to step in the shower."

She waved a hand in the air as if she couldn't care less that he'd be in the other room—naked.

Deb applied the drugstore cosmetics with a heavy hand. The foundation changed her skin tone down to her décolletage. She stroked on black mascara, eyeliner and three different shades of eye shadow until an unfamiliar pair of deep-set smoky eyes stared back at her from the mirror. The coral blush she feathered onto her cheekbones altered the contours of her face. She'd save the lipstick until after she slipped into her dress.

The water from the shower had stopped at about the same time Deb had finished her eyes.

As she turned from the mirror, Beau burst from the bathroom with his arms spread. "Well?"

He'd purchased his own wig—dark hair brushed back from his forehead with the hint of a widow's peak. He'd changed his blue eyes with dark contacts, just like hers, and a bushy moustache and beard covered the lower half of his face.

He would look almost nerdy if it weren't for all those muscles on display above the towel wrapped around his waist.

"Wow, you sort of look like a scientist."

His mouth formed an O amid all that hair. "And you look sort of amazing in a mistress-of-the-dark kind of way."

"Too much?" She bit her lip. She didn't want to stand out in the crowd.

"It'll work. Zendaris wouldn't even be able to pick you out."

"If he's there. I don't think he'll show his face."

"I think we can both show ours without being recognized."

"Wouldn't you want Dr. Herndon to recognize you?"

"There are other ways I can make myself known."

Which he obviously wasn't going to tell her about. She pulled the heavy dress from the hanger. "I'm going to put this thing on. Are you done in the bathroom?"

"You don't have to get dressed in the bathroom. We can just turn our backs to each other. I have to get into my monkey suit, too."

Deb staked out one corner of the room while Beau staked out the other. Did he find her modesty juvenile? Little did he know she had a hard time controlling her thoughts when confronted with his half-clothed body.

She untied the robe and let it drop to the floor. She stepped into the dress and tugged the bodice over her breasts. "Can you zip this for me?"

"My pleasure." His warm fingers skimmed her bare back as he pulled the dress together and tugged on the zipper. "There's a little hook at the top. Might take me a minute to get it with my clumsy fingers."

He could take more than a few minutes if that meant she could continue feeling the warmth emanating from his body and inhaling his clean, masculine scent.

"There." He placed his hands on her shoulders

and turned her toward him. His dark eyes kindled, a different light from his usual blue fire—but it still melted her insides.

"You look stunning."

She gave a half laugh and stepped back, almost tripping on her gown. "It's the makeup. Men always claim they like a woman with a fresh, natural face and then go all gaga over the woman with the artfully applied makeup."

"I go gaga over you, natural or made-up."

"Yeah, well, we tried that before." She brushed past him to get her heels from the closet. "Didn't work out that great."

He appeared behind her in a flash as she lifted her skirt to slip a foot into her shoe.

"It didn't? I always thought it worked out pretty great. I had no regrets. Did you?"

Balancing on one high heel, she gripped the closet door frame as she put on the other shoe. When she'd discovered her pregnancy, that night loomed as a disaster. But once she'd held Bobby in her arms, she wouldn't have changed one moment of it although her son had never had a father.

If Beau knew the outcome of their brief encounter, he wouldn't think it had worked out so great.

"I—I just mean we never saw each other after that. I didn't even know how to contact you." She had her excuse for not telling him about Bobby if it ever came to that.

He brushed her hair from her back, holding the heavy strands of the wig in one hand. "If you had known how to contact me, would you have done so?"

She whipped around and her hair slid from his grasp. With the five-inch heels on, she could almost glare at him eye to eye. "You knew who I was. Why didn't you ever contact me?"

He parted his fingers across his moustache and around his mouth. "We didn't exactly discuss our next date, did we?"

"It wasn't the time or the place."

"Exactly. Don't forget, Deb. You were the one who slipped out at the crack of dawn, leaving me with nothing more than a scribbled note and the scent of you all over those sheets."

With his words, the memory of that night slammed against her full-force and she grabbed the closet again and closed her eyes. "I did leave you the note."

He chuckled. "Just like a woman to expect a man to figure out something from that. That note made me think you saw that as a one-nighter, and hey, if that's all I could get, I could die a happy man. But I didn't figure you wanted any follow-up, and I guess I was right since you had a boyfriend or a lover at the time—Bobby's dad."

"I'm sorry." She clasped her hands over her aching heart.

"No need to apologize." He chucked her under the chin and crossed back to his side of the room. "Now I can die a happy man."

"Don't talk about dying." She dipped her head and fussed with the skirt of her dress.

He slipped his feet into a pair of shiny black dress shoes and shrugged into his cummerbund. "Can you help me with the bow tie?"

"Of course." She flexed her fingers and he returned to her realm just when she'd gotten her breath back. His proximity made her pulse race and her skin prickle with heat.

She wanted to correct his false impression that she'd had a lover stashed away somewhere else the night she'd met him. But to do so would be to confess that he was Bobby's father. She wasn't ready for that yet—and neither was he.

They had to rescue Bobby first.

He tilted his chin up as she tied the bow tie, and his fake beard tickled her fingers. She straightened the ends of the bow tie and then smoothed her hands across the front of his starched shirt. "There you go."

"Perfect." He sidled in front of the mirror, but his gaze shifted to her. "Why *did* Bobby's father let you and Bobby go?"

"It's a long story suited for another time and

another place." And that had to be the understatement of the evening.

He shrugged his broad shoulders and stepped around her to rummage in another bag. "And now the pièce de résistance."

He perched a pair of dark-framed glasses on the end of his nose, and she laughed.

Running a hand over his slicked-back hair, he said, "Overkill?"

She shook her head. "It's just that the way that tux fits you, you're going to be the hottest absent-minded professor at that shindig."

His grin only served to emphasize her point. "Ladies first. You take a taxi to the Grand Marquis, I'll follow in another taxi and I'll see you at the party."

She swept up her beaded clutch from the bed and hugged it to her chest. "Shouldn't I have some kind of weapon?"

"You're not going to kill Dr. Herndon."

"Yes, but don't I need a prop or something? I have to make some kind of show of it."

His eyebrows rose above the top of his thick frames. "Show of what? Do you want to get arrested for attempted murder?"

"What if you don't make it inside?"

"I'll make it inside."

"Damn it." Deb stamped her foot and the black dress rustled around her legs. "I feel like I'm going into a boxing ring with no gloves. Zendaris is expecting me to kill Dr. Herndon, and I don't even know what the plan is."

"Technically—" Beau curled both hands around her throat and wedged his thumbs beneath her chin "—you're still my captive. I'm going out on a limb trusting you, but I don't know your real intentions. You're on the edge, and there's no telling what you might do to get your son back."

She jerked away from his warm touch, dashing a tear from the corner of her eye. "I don't like feeling helpless."

"Trust me. I'll handle this."

"You expect me to trust you and yet you just admitted you can't trust me?" She dug her heels into the carpet.

"You lied to me."

She blinked. *He knew.* "Wh-what are you talking about?"

"When I first approached you, you lied about having contact with Zendaris."

It took a few seconds for the pounding in her temples to subside. "Of course I lied. My son's life was on the line."

"It still is."

She jabbed her finger just below his perfectly tweaked bow tie. "Don't screw this up."

"I never do."

"And that's a lie." She curved her lipsticked

mouth into a smile. "You screwed up this assignment for Prospero, didn't you? They expect you to serve them my head on a platter."

He tugged on the lapels of his jacket. "Don't be so sure I won't."

THE TAXI ZIPPED through the streets of Boston on the way to the Marquis while Deb's fingers toyed with the beads on her black evening clutch. She could wipe the smirk right off Beau's face if she told him the truth.

That wasn't a sufficient reason to tell him that he was Bobby's father, but she did have to tell him. He deserved to know. What he did with that information rested with him.

Not all fathers wanted to be part of their children's lives. Not all mothers wanted to be part of their children's lives. For the second time that night, she whisked a tear away from her mascaraed lashes.

She'd dealt with her abandonment issues long ago, but she didn't want Bobby to deal with the same issues. At least he had a mother who loved him, which was more than she could claim. But she'd had Robert, and in the end that had been enough.

Her taxi joined a row of them lined up in front of the Marquis.

"Do you want me to drop you here, or wait until I roll up to the entrance?"

"This is fine." The hand that reached into her bag for some cash had a slight tremble. She wished she knew how Beau planned to pull this off.

The driver had hopped out of the taxi and opened the door for her. Must be the dress. She pressed the money into his hand and thanked him.

Closing her eyes, she rubbed her lips together. Time to don her identity for the night. She couldn't be a nervous mom planning an assassination. That person wouldn't win her many friends.

She joined the throng of people entering the hotel, hitched up the bodice of her dress and patted the sides of her breasts to make sure they didn't spill out. Then she put on a smile and plucked her invitation from her clutch.

Lifting the skirt of her dress, she stepped onto the escalator. Tuxedoed men formed a barrier at the entrance to the ballroom, scanning invitations and checking bags. Without a metal detector in sight, it would've been easy to slip a weapon in here.

She huffed out a sigh and presented her ticket to the sentry. He waved her through, and the crowd sucked her into the room.

She claimed a glass of champagne from a passing tray and tossed back half of the bubbly liquid. Then she threaded her way through taffeta, silk and brocade all scented with expensive perfumes, and zeroed in on a clutch of people at the corner of the food table. Who didn't like talking about food?

She elbowed her way up to the trough and stabbed a shrimp with a red plastic toothpick and held it up to her neighbor. "Have you tried any of the dipping sauces yet?"

Her new friend tapped a silver dish. "Try the Thai peanut sauce."

That remark launched an exchange about allergies, the weather, the Red Sox and Anthrax. Feeling warmed up, Deb sidled up to the next group where more inane conversation bubbled from her lips.

Facing the ballroom's entrance, she tracked the new arrivals. She could pick out Dr. Herndon from a newspaper photo but not from this crowd.

Her gaze skimmed over a tall man with a full beard and moustache and then backtracked. She released a pent-up breath. Beau had made it through the doors.

He jerked his head around as if knowing she had him in her crosshairs. His dark eyes behind the thick glasses met hers, and he cut a swath through the crowd toward the bar.

She had a sudden longing to swill something stronger than the sweet champagne making the rounds. She excused herself from her current circle and weaved through a pack of penguins to join Beau at the bar.

"Big crowd, isn't it?"

"Scotch, neat, please." Beau barely turned his head. "It is."

"I'm not sure I can even pick out the guest of honor." She rapped her knuckles on the bar. "Make that two, please."

Beau curled his long fingers around his glass and moved away from the bar. She followed, but she stood apart from him and scanned the room.

"Over by the stage."

She glanced at the end of the room where several band members were tuning their instruments. "Tall man, receding hairline, jaunty polka-dot bow tie?"

"That's receding?" He smoothed a hand over his wig. "Go get acquainted as the black-haired siren. He likes pretty women. You need to get him alone."

"How am I going to manage that? He has a million people around him."

"Use your assets." His gaze dropped to her décolletage.

She nodded. This wasn't the first time as a female agent she'd used her sex appeal on a mission—but it might be her last if she couldn't get this job done.

She lolled a tiny sip of scotch on her tongue before letting it roll down her throat, leaving a trail of fire. She straightened her shoulders, not bothering to tug at her dress's bodice this time.

Sauntering toward the stage, she rolled her hips and twirled a lock of black hair around one finger. Herndon noticed her approach from five feet away and broke off his conversation to send a smile of encouragement her way.

She tripped to a stop at the stage, and her drink sloshed up the side of her glass. She put one finger in her mouth to suck off the scotch and widened her eyes. "Is there going to be music and dancing?"

Herndon's Adam's apple bobbed once. "There is. Do you dance, Miss…?"

He held out a hand, and Deb leaned in close to clasp it. "Desiree—it's like *desire* with an extra *e* at the end—and I love to dance."

Herndon chuckled and his hand, which had grown moist, tightened its grip on hers. "I do, too. Promise you'll find me when the band strikes up the first tune."

"Absolutely, Dr. Herndon."

"You know who I am?"

"Of course." She winked. "You're the man of the hour, aren't you?"

His smile stretched from ear to ear. "I'm flattered, Desiree, and please call me Scott. I'm going to get a refill, but look me up for the first song."

She wet her mouth with the scotch and then swept her tongue over her lips. "Of course, Scott."

She turned and walked away, feeling Dr. Herndon's eyes pinned to her swaying hips. Was he going to feel stupid when he found out her true identity? Probably not when he discovered she'd spared his life.

On her way to the ladies' room, she shot a look at Beau, chatting with two serious-looking young men. He ignored her.

She scuttled into the bathroom and hunched over the vanity. She didn't like using sex to do her job, but even a renowned scientist like Dr. Herndon wasn't immune to female flattery and charms. Was that her fault?

He wouldn't be so anxious to go off with her if she presented as a studious young woman interested in nuclear physics. She'd go for the kill after their dance and invite him outside for some fresh air.

Beau would probably make his case then.

She grabbed a silver tube of lipstick from her bag and smoothed it over her lips.

The toilet in one of the occupied stalls flushed,

and a woman squeezed through the stall door, flattening the flared skirt of her gown.

She joined Deb at the vanity and caught her eye in the mirror. "Sexy dress, but you might want to watch that bodice before it becomes a sexy half dress."

Deb glanced down at the top of her dress, hugging the curves of her breasts in a desperate attempt to stay up. "Oh, thanks."

She yanked at the bodice for the hundredth time that night, but once out of the bathroom she tugged it down to its previous daring level. Her slipping bodice just might be the key to getting Dr. Herndon outside…and saving his life.

Several minutes later, melodious chords rose from the dais and Deb made a beeline for Dr. Herndon, surrounded by adoring geeks.

Dipping between the black-clad shoulders, she shook her finger at Dr. Herndon. "You promised."

Like a magnet, his gaze dropped to her cleavage. He foisted his empty glass on one of his fans and rubbed his hands together. "I was waiting for you, Desiree."

He crooked his elbow, and she slipped her hand around his arm. He led her to the dance floor where several couples were already swirling to a waltz.

His arm dropped to her waist and he pulled her close, crushing her barely concealed breasts against his starched shirt. His heartbeat rat-tatted against her chest, his warmth heating her skin.

Ugh, he must be very excited. She bit her lip and muttered a curse at Beau Slater.

He twirled her once and stumbled as he hugged her close again.

"Are you okay, Scott?"

He wheezed. "I'm fine. Haven't danced in a while and it's a bit warm in here, don't you think?"

He couldn't have offered her a more perfect setup.

She squirmed out of his tight grip and smiled into his red face. "I *am* feeling overheated. Maybe we can get a breath of fresh air outside."

"Let's finish this waltz and it's a deal." A trickle of sweat rolled down the side of his face and dripped onto his high collar.

"Are you sure you're okay, Scott? We can sit this one out and get that air right now."

His lips moved but no sound came out. Instead, a trickle of saliva dribbled to his chin.

"Are you ill?" Great—all she needed was for Dr. Herndon to draw attention to himself.

His fingers dug into her flesh and his knees buckled. She wrested away from his hold so he wouldn't take her down with him. And down he went.

As Deb hovered over him, he clutched his

throat with both hands. Blood gushed from his mouth and he toppled over.

A woman screamed.

Deb stepped back from the blood pooling on the dance floor.

Someone grabbed her arm.

Several people crouched beside Dr. Herndon.

One solemn-faced man looked up and said to no one in particular, "Dr. Herndon is dead."

Chapter Eight

"Let's go." Beau tugged on Deb's arm again. She was the last one to have contact with Dr. Herndon, and she didn't need the police questioning her.

She stumbled against him, and he had to pull her dress up before she spilled out of it. No wonder Dr. Herndon had been so captivated. Now he was dead. Had she done it?

He led her through the crowd pressing in to see the dead man on the floor lying in a pool of blood that had spewed from his mouth. Poison.

Two security guards rushed past them. Shouts and cries swirled through the ballroom.

And still Beau fought against the tide to escape from the room. Once outside the ballroom, he hustled Deb toward the stairwell.

"It's just one floor. Can you make it?"

She hiked up her skirts and made a dainty dash for the stairs like Cinderella after the ball. Only Cinderella hadn't left any dead bodies behind.

Beau pushed through the fire door and pulled Deb out after him. The cold air blasted his face, bringing tears to his eyes. He took one step toward the line of taxis and limos at the curb and then flattened his body against the wall, taking Deb with him.

Emergency vehicles double-parked alongside the taxis, and the first responders surged into the hotel.

Holding on to Deb's hand, Beau pivoted and walked quickly in the other direction from the commotion. He grabbed the handle of a taxi door and stuffed Deb into the backseat—right after he yanked the black wig from her head and the beard from his face.

He gave the driver the name of their hotel and collapsed against the seat. His gaze slid to Deb, her chest rising and falling, wisps of auburn hair framing her face. He pressed a finger to his lips.

When they got to the hotel, they stood shivering on the sidewalk. He turned her toward the door. "You go through the lobby, and I'll go the back way."

He took the three flights of stairs two at a time. By the time he reached the room, Deb had the chain on the door.

She let him into the room and then dropped onto the bed, the black dress swirling around her.

"Did you do it? Did you kill Dr. Herndon?"

She popped up like a jack-in-the-box. "Are you crazy? Of course I didn't kill him."

All the tension he'd been carrying in his shoulders seeped out—almost all of it. "Okay, okay."

"Do you really think I'm capable of murdering someone?"

"You're a covert ops agent. You'll do what's necessary to get the job done. You're also a mom who wants her son back."

"I'm not a cold-blooded killer."

"What happened back there?"

"Poison."

"My take exactly, but how? Why? Who?"

"I don't know." Her fingers pleated the silky black material of her dress. "Everything was going as planned. I had Dr. Herndon wrapped around my finger. He would've followed me to Jupiter after that dance."

"So would've half the men in that room."

Her glance knifed him between the eyes, and he spread his hands. "That's a good thing. You were doing your job. When did you notice he wasn't right?"

"Almost as soon as we hit the dance floor—rapid heartbeat, sweating, flushed skin." She hugged herself. "He became unresponsive and then collapsed to the floor."

"It didn't look like anyone else was affected, so someone targeted him, but how?"

"His drink. He seemed to be drinking a lot. His glass was always empty or almost empty. Someone must've slipped him something in his drink."

"It couldn't have been Zendaris. He fully expected you to do the deed."

"What if he knew I wouldn't do it? He wanted Dr. Herndon dead, so he had a backup plan." She pulled the pins from her hair and they fell to the bed. "What if he knows I failed?"

"How could he know your thought processes? If he had a plant at the party, he must've noticed you moving in on Herndon."

She doubled over and her now-loose hair tumbled around her bare shoulders. "What a mess."

"Deb?"

Peering at him through a veil of hair, she said, "Yes?"

"It's not a mess."

"Dr. Herndon is dead."

"Exactly."

She sucked in her plump lower lip. "I didn't kill him. I wouldn't kill him."

"Zendaris doesn't know that. All Zendaris is going to see on the news tomorrow is that Dr. Scott Herndon died at the party in his honor. Don't get me wrong." He peeled off his jacket and loosened the bow tie. "I'm sorry for Dr. Herndon, but his murder leaves you in the clear."

"That's…awful."

"But true."

"Do you really think Zendaris will believe I murdered Dr. Herndon?"

"Why wouldn't he? He's holding your son. He sent you to do a job. The target has been neutralized."

"But who did it?"

"Maybe someone who has the same objective as Zendaris. Maybe the same person who shot at you the other night."

She plowed her fingers through her hair and pressed her palms against her temples. "Is there some shadow operation going on paralleling mine? This *is* a mess. If someone gets to the anti-drone plans before I do, what reason will Zendaris have for returning Bobby?"

"We'll just have to beat them to it." His cummerbund gaped open and he shrugged out if it.

"How are we going to do that? I don't even know what Zendaris wants."

"You know, Deb. He wants the plans, and somehow Dr. Herndon was involved."

"Was." She shivered.

Beau knelt before her and slipped the high heels from her feet. "You did good, Cinderella."

"I used my body to entice a world-renowned scientist." She flopped back on the bed and her toes dangled just above the floor.

"You did what you had to do." He took one slender foot in his hand and massaged her instep. "You did what was required. That's what we do. It's our number one job requirement."

She hitched up on her elbows. "Do you ever get tired of it? Do you ever get tired of being Loki?"

"Sure I do." He sat back on his heels and pulled her foot onto his thigh. "But it's what I signed up for. If I had wanted to settle down in some cramped house with six kids and work nine to five every day, I would've followed in my dad's footsteps. I, too, could've worked in the family business eighty hours a week."

Her still-brown eyes glittered and he jerked back from the sparks of anger there. Why did she care if he spurned his parents' lifestyle? She'd changed since having a kid, but he supposed that was natural. Kids changed you. He saw it over and over with his friends. Not. For. Him.

"Don't get me wrong." He released her foot. "I love my folks and my older brother who stayed to help Dad with the business and will eventually take it over. I love my nieces and nephews. All nine of them—ten, my younger sister just had a baby."

"It sounds—" she swiped a hand beneath her nose "—amazing. To have all that family around."

"You know, it is." A smile tugged at his mouth.

"One of my nephews cracks me up. He's always asking the most off-the-wall questions, and one of my nieces is a total tomboy. She plays just as rough as her male cousins, but her sister is a princess who won't wear anything but pink."

Hunching forward, she said, "It sounds like you know them well, like you pay attention to them as people."

"Is that surprising? They are people—each one with a unique personality." He jumped to his feet and brushed off his slacks. "You gotta see that with your own son, even though he's only…"

"Two." She rose from the bed. "Bobby is almost two."

Beau drew his brows over his nose. Hadn't they been together three years ago? She hadn't wasted any time going back to her lover. He tightened his jaw. "I'm going to get out of this monkey suit and hit the sack. Mission accomplished."

"Man dead."

"You had nothing to do with that. Let's just hope Zendaris thinks you did."

The following morning, voices from the TV intruded on Deb's hazy dreams. She burrowed under the pillow, but that failed when Beau started tugging on her feet.

"Deb, wake up. Wake up. It's on the news."

She rolled over and sat up, squinting at the images on the TV. A reporter was standing in front of the Grand Marquis, yapping into a microphone.

"What's he saying? Are they calling it a murder?"

"The Boston P.D. is going to wait for the autopsy and the toxicology report before making any kind of statement."

She grabbed the remote from the foot of the bed and increased the volume.

A blonde news anchor appeared on the split screen with the reporter. "Do the police have any reason to believe this is foul play, Dave?"

"No, Charlotte, but they are looking for this woman."

The room spun and Deb grabbed the bedspread in her fists as she stared at a grainy photo of herself entering the Marquis Hotel, her black wig hiding half of her face. "Oh, my God."

"She was the person dancing with Dr. Herndon when he collapsed. The police would like to talk to her."

"I bet they would." Beau dropped on the bed next to her. "Don't worry. Nobody is going to link you with that picture."

"Maybe whoever poisoned Dr. Herndon was smart enough to make it look like an accident." She scooted back toward the headboard. "That's what I would've done."

He lifted an eyebrow in her direction and

clicked off the TV. "Let's just hope Zendaris saw the same report."

Deb reached for the phone charging on the nightstand. "Nothing yet."

"You must be more than ready for breakfast after skipping dinner last night, unless you filled up on the appetizers at the party."

She wrinkled her nose. "I had one shrimp and after what happened to Dr. Herndon, I'm glad I didn't eat anything else."

"I'll head down to the hotel restaurant and meet you there." He turned with his hand on the doorknob. "Unless you want me to wait for you. I know you're a Prospero agent, Deb, but you're off your game. If you don't want to be left on your own…"

"I want my weapon." She leveled a finger at the closet, housing the room safe where Beau had stashed her .45.

"Fifty-one, ninety-eight."

Before the door even closed behind him, Deb scrambled off the bed and flew to the closet. She tried the combination and a red Open flashed on the display.

She swung open the door and lifted her gun from the safe. She checked the chamber and blew out a breath. Now she could handle anything.

She took the gun with her into the bathroom while she showered and dressed. Returning to the room, she scooped up the gown puddled on the floor where she'd dropped it last night. Shaking it out, she noticed a couple of shiny spots on the skirt.

Gathering the material in her hands, she brought it close to her face and gasped. Blood—dried blood. She stuffed the dress in the closet and slid the mirrored door closed.

If she had gotten Dr. Herndon outside sooner last night, could she have saved his life? She had no way of knowing. When had someone slipped him the poison? How quickly had the poison acted?

Fate had taken over last night, and it had been Dr. Herndon's time to die.

She stashed her weapon in her bag and left the room to join Beau. She could escape now if she wanted. Nothing stood in her way. She had her gun and the phone connecting her to Zendaris—and her son.

But she was fooling herself if she didn't believe Loki would find her. She hadn't even known he'd been tailing her the first time. What had he said earlier? She was off her game. Yeah, she'd given up the game completely when Zendaris had snatched Bobby.

That wasn't the real reason she didn't bolt. Beau made her feel safe, protected, like she had a chance, like Bobby had a chance.

And then there was the paternity issue.

He'd made it clear last night he didn't have kids in his five-year plan. He'd spoken of his siblings and nieces and nephews in such an off-hand manner, but with such warmth. That part gave her hope.

When the elevator opened on the lobby, she sighed and flipped her ponytail over her shoulder. She'd kill to have a large chaotic family like that.

She spotted the top half of Beau's face above a newspaper, and weaved through the tables to sit across from him.

He lowered the paper when she pulled out the chair.

"Still just on coffee?"

"I didn't want to get ahead of you." He snapped the paper in his hands. "And I wanted to read the coverage of last night."

"Big deal?"

"Oh, yeah."

"What's the tone of the article?"

He folded the paper and tucked it under a menu. "The reporter is being cautious, but *foul play* practically screams from every other line in the story."

"Is anyone speculating on a motive—anyone but us, that is?"

"There's a lot about the symposium and who had a vested interest in the discussions."

"No mention of Nico Zendaris?"

He swirled his coffee. "There never is, is there?"

"We—" she cleared her throat "—Prospero wants to change that—shine a spotlight on him and his organization."

"You're still part of Prospero, Deb." He put a finger on a plastic menu and slid it toward her. "The work you're doing now will benefit Prospero."

"Honestly, Beau, I just want to benefit Bobby. I want him home with me."

"I know." He covered her hand with his. "It must be tough. I can't even imagine what one of my sisters would do if her child was missing, or my brothers for that matter."

Or you? Could you imagine what you'd do if a dangerous arms dealer had your son?

Folding her hands in her lap, she looked down. She couldn't even meet his eyes anymore when talking about Bobby. She had to tell him, but she'd waited so long now it would seem as if she were just trying to light a fire under him to rescue Bobby. He might not even believe her at this point.

"Do me a favor, Deb, and eat. In fact, I should've made that a condition of returning your weapon." He flipped the menu open in front of her.

"Why did you return it? With my gun back

in my possession and my first task for Zendaris completed, I could've hightailed it out of here and finished the work on my own."

He shrugged. "I didn't think there was much danger of that."

"Really?" She didn't like the sound of this. When people like Loki failed to see her as a threat, she'd definitely lost her edge.

The waitress stopped by the table, took their order and filled their coffee cups.

When she left, Beau folded his hands around his cup. "We're on the same side now. I want to help you get Bobby back. I want to help you get your life back, whether or not that's with Prospero."

Or you?

The words came out of left field and she covered her mouth with one hand as if she'd uttered them aloud. When did she ever believe she'd have a life with Beau? He was committed to life on the road, a rootless existence that didn't tie him down to the drudgery of family and hearth and home.

He'd had all of that with his big warm middle-class family. And he'd rejected it.

"Why? Why are you so willing to help me when you could've bagged me at that hotel and had me back at Prospero headquarters a few hours later? You could've collected your bonus, which I'm sure Jack was offering for a speedy delivery, and been on to your next assignment."

"Obviously, I need to give you more reassurance." He held up the index finger of one hand and reached into his back pocket with the other. He flipped open his wallet and a plastic insert cascaded down to the table.

Children of different ages, some babies, some toothless, some freckled and towheaded grinned at her from the shiny plastic. "The ten nieces and nephews?"

"Nine. I haven't put the newest one in the lineup yet."

Deb trailed her finger along the smiling faces and halted at one blond boy who made her heart skip a beat. "Who's this one?"

"That's Grant. He's my brother's boy."

Deb gulped. Grant could be Bobby's twin. Hadn't Beau seen the resemblance between her own son and his nephew? Or had he just seen a scared boy who looked tired?

God, Bobby had looked tired. Were they feeding him properly? Drugging him?

Her appetite evaporated, and she released the plastic insert. It swung over the table like a pendulum. "Cute kids."

"I'm sorry. That was probably an insensitive thing to do."

"Not at all. You want to help me and Bobby

because my son reminds you of your nieces and nephews. I get it."

He cocked his head and two vertical lines formed between his eyebrows. "Reminds me? I don't know your son, but any child in danger is gonna tug at my heartstrings. Are you surprised I have heartstrings? Whatever those are. Are you surprised Loki has a heart?"

"I know Loki has a heart. I fell asleep to it beating beneath my cheek that night."

A smile played around his mouth as the waitress delivered their food. When she left, he squirted some ketchup on his plate and his smile widened. "I thought reference to that night was off-limits."

"It's going to come up, isn't it?" *And it's so much more important than you know, Beau.* "It happened. We saw each other in the buff, we made love, we shared the shower."

"Stop." He made a cross in the air with his fork and knife. "I'm going to attempt to eat my breakfast without drooling."

She grinned and attacked her own plate. On one level she wanted to feel sad and anxious over Bobby every minute of the day to keep her focus, but on another, with Beau to lighten her load, she felt human and more capable of being the kind of mother Bobby needed right now.

The kind of mother who could kick ass.

Then the white elephant on the table, the cell phone from Zendaris, buzzed twice. Deb wiped her hands on her napkin and hit the button to read the incoming text.

Beau hunched forward, his silverware clattering in his plate. "What's it say?"

She turned the phone toward him. "Good kill."

Chapter Nine

"That's a good thing, Deb." He nodded once and dug into his omelet, not wanting to acknowledge Zendaris's power to rattle Deb. "He believes you killed Dr. Herndon. That's what we want."

"But what does he want?" She dropped the phone on the table and tapped it. "Why the cryptic message? Why doesn't he just tell me what to do?"

"Because he's toying with you. Don't let him get under your skin. That's exactly what he wants."

She choked and gulped her coffee. "He has my son. That's about as far as someone can get under my skin."

"He'll tell you what to do next, don't worry. And when he does—" Beau stabbed a chunk of potato and held it up "—you're going to have another demand for him."

"I am?"

"You're in the driver's seat right now. You

killed a man. You just showed you're tough enough. Now he needs to deliver on his end before you proceed."

"Bobby. I want to see Bobby again, make sure he's okay."

"This time you're going to talk to Bobby. He's going to have to put him on the phone and let you hear his voice."

Beau's words filled Deb with strength. She didn't like feeling helpless. Who did? But for her, those vulnerable feelings sucked her back to her childhood, before Robert had come into her life like a guardian angel.

She didn't want to go back to that dark place again. Now here was another guardian angel in the unlikely form of a tall, lean, dangerous spy. And he gave her hope and courage. That's what Bobby needed right now.

"Bring it on, Zendaris." She flicked the phone with her fingers. Then she finished her breakfast—every last bite.

On the way up to the room, Beau asked, "Do you want to work out at the gym with me?"

She stopped at the door. "How did you know that's exactly what I needed?"

Placing his hands on her shoulders, he dug his fingers into the base of her neck, sending shivers down her back. He knew exactly what she needed.

"I think it's time for you to get your mojo back."

"Is that why you returned my gun?"

"That and the fact that someone is running around Boston who seems to be on the same track as you. You need to be able to protect yourself."

She turned toward the door with Beau's hands still on her shoulders and slipped her card in the slot. "What if Zendaris finds out that someone else killed Dr. Herndon?"

"That's not going to happen. Why would it unless the killer himself tells Zendaris? I don't think he's going to want to broadcast that because Zendaris will see him as a rival. And we know what Zendaris does to rivals."

Once in the room, Deb changed into some makeshift workout clothes—her jeans from yesterday and a T-shirt and tennis shoes.

Beau put on the shorts and T-shirt he'd worn to the gym before and plucked the material of the shirt from his chest. "If Zendaris keeps you dangling much longer, I'm going to have to go home and pack a bag."

"Where is home?"

"An apartment in D.C."

"We don't live far from each other. I have a small house in the burbs of Virginia." To think all this time, Bobby had been close to his father. It would be convenient once Beau knew. He and

Bobby could see each other. He could spend time with Bobby between assignments.

She slid a glance at Beau as he punched the elevator button. "I—I suppose a house in the suburbs sounds like torture to you."

"To me, but a kid needs that. Kids need space and greenery and—" he waved his arm "—all that stuff."

"All the stuff you had and didn't appreciate."

He leaned a shoulder against the inside of the elevator car. "Who said I didn't appreciate it?"

"What would you call it, then? By your own account, you graduated from high school, enlisted in the Marines and started training for the most dangerous missions."

"I'd call it—" he swiped his card to unlock the door to the gym "—a thirst for adventure."

"And have you slaked that thirst yet?" She grabbed a towel from the counter and hung it over her shoulder.

"Did you slake yours?"

She spread her towel on a bench and straddled it. "It wasn't a matter of slaking. I didn't have a choice. I have a son to care for, so I had to scale back."

"Exactly." He ran a hand along a row of dumbbells and grabbed one, hoisting it from its cradle. "When circumstances change, you make the necessary changes in your life."

He curled the weight up to his shoulder. "Now are you going to keep talking or pump some iron?"

She snorted. "My friend and I back home can do both."

"Men just grunt."

They continued to work out, exchanging snippets of conversation and a few grunts.

Deb stretched out on a mat, feeling a pleasant ache in her muscles. A workout couldn't relieve all her stress, but it had helped.

Then the cell phone buzzed.

She snatched it up and glanced at Beau doing flys on a machine. A few other guests had joined them in the gym, so she didn't want to yell across the floor.

She answered the phone. "Yes?"

The hated voice purred in her ear. "Good job, Deb. I knew the agents of Prospero Team Three were killers, and you didn't disappoint."

"We didn't know your wife was there."

A sharp intake of air was all the answer he gave. Then he cleared his throat. "The assassination of Dr. Herndon was just one step. Are you ready for the next?"

"Wait. I can't talk here." She scrambled from the mat and waved to Beau. She pointed to the covered patio off the gym floor, and he followed her out.

She mouthed *Zendaris*.

"Okay. I'm ready for the next step if you are."

Zendaris paused. "What are you talking about?"

"I want to talk to my son. You showed me the picture, and I killed Herndon for you. Now I want to talk to him."

"He's a toddler. He doesn't talk much."

Anger thumped against the back of her head and she took a deep breath. "He's my son. I want to hear his voice."

"I have a son, too, Deb. Prospero knows that now after capturing my children's nanny."

"You mean the nanny you left for dead? Yes, we know you have a son and a daughter." She'd appeal to his fatherly instincts but he probably didn't have any. "So you know two-year-olds can talk, and I want to talk to mine."

Beau was nodding encouragement.

Zendaris gave an exaggerated sigh. "You're getting to be more trouble than you're worth."

"I won't do one more task until I speak to my son."

"I'll arrange it, but once I do you're mine."

"I'll do your dirty work because you have my son, but I'll never be yours."

WHILE DEB TOOK a shower, Beau clicked on the TV to see if there were any more news stories about Dr. Herndon's death, but the local news wasn't on yet and the story wasn't big enough for the national news channel to carry it.

He'd been proud of Deb today. She seemed to be getting her spine back, although he couldn't fault her for losing it in the first place. Even if one of his nieces or nephews had been snatched, he would've gone nuts.

Deb must really like kids. She'd probably like more than one. She seemed really interested in the pictures of his family. He must've come across as a real jerk the night they'd met if she believed he took his family for granted. Nothing could be further from the truth.

Had he gotten his taste for thrills and chills out of his system? He'd experienced more than a lifetime of them, enough to write three books. But the woman he settled with would have to be special—just that right mix of independence and femininity. He hadn't met her yet.

Until that night in Zurich when he'd seen Deb down the length of that bar.

For the longest time, he'd convinced himself it was all about the great sex, the hot chemistry between them. But he'd come to realize Deb possessed all the qualities necessary to lure him in like a magnet. Spending time with her again, even under these circumstances or maybe especially under these circumstances, reinforced his belief that she had something unique, some combination of traits and beliefs that matched up with his.

Could he let her go after this assignment?

His laptop in the corner beeped, and he strolled to it and hit a key to wake it up.

The search for the identity of the man at the bookstore had concluded and a file had been deposited on his desktop.

He double-clicked on the file, and a document popped open containing pictures and corresponding text—a who's who of bad guys.

A sweet scent wafted from behind and he cranked his head over his shoulder to take in Deb massaging lotion into her hands.

"Is the search program done?"

"Yep. Returned quite a few possibilities for our bookstore patron."

"Can we look now, or did you want to get something to eat first?"

"The sandwich I grabbed on the way up to the room is enough." He spun the laptop toward her and pulled up the other chair. "Let's have a look."

They scanned through several faces, reading their criminal bios and taking a few notes on the hotel stationery.

"Anyone look familiar?"

"Prospero has had our sights on a few of these people, so I'm going to eliminate those guys right now. Nobody we looked at had ties to Zendaris. Has to be someone off our radar."

After an hour and a half, they'd narrowed their search down to five men—all the size and shape of the man at the bookstore.

Beau tapped the screen. "I'm going to do some more research on these guys. If we can locate our man, there's no telling what we'll discover."

"Like where they're holding Bobby."

"Exactly." He accessed another classified database and fed information on their five suspects into it.

Deb sat on the bed, crossing her legs beneath her. "Aren't some alarm bells going to go off somewhere when you input data into those systems?"

"Definitely."

"Will the usage be tracked back to you?"

"I have an excuse. I'm on assignment, so while someone may be tracking my search criteria in these databases, it shouldn't raise any suspicions. I use these all the time. What's the difference now?"

"The difference is you've gone to the dark side. You've joined forces with your prey."

He hit the final key and stood up to stretch. "As far as anyone knows, I'm still tracking a suspected rogue Prospero agent."

"I hope so." She plucked at the bedspread with

nervous fingers. "Dinner in the hotel again or room service?"

"I'm sick of this hotel. Let's go out."

"Disguises?"

"Not the brunette from last night and not the blonde from the jewelry store. It seems that every identity you have gets into trouble. You're better off with your natural hair color."

"I was no brunette last night—that was more mistress of the dark."

"Boston P.D.'s looking for mistress of the dark now, so you'd better not bring her back."

The phone that Deb kept by her side buzzed, and her face paled just like it did every time a call or text came through. This time it was a call.

She licked her lips and answered it.

As always, she put it on speaker, and a gruff voice scratched over the line. "You ready for the kid?"

At least they knew Zendaris was probably not holding Bobby himself. Beau pressed the record button on his mini recorder.

Deb's voice, strong and sure, answered, "Yes."

More shuffling and scratching came over the line and the man's voice barked, "He's listening."

"Bobby? Bobby, is that you? It's Mommy."

A child's voice responded, "Mommy?"

"Are you okay, Bobby? Mommy misses you and will see you soon."

"Mommy, I wanna go home."

Deb squeezed her eyes shut and Beau had a strong urge to take her pain away.

"You will. Soon, Bobby. Are you getting enough to eat?"

"Ice cream."

"You're eating ice cream?" She rolled her eyes at Beau.

"'Cuz my throat hurts. I'm tired."

"Bobby, are you sick?"

"Throat hurts. Bye, Mommy."

"Bobby? Bobby?"

"He's done. Kids this age don't talk much."

Deb had slid to the floor with her back leaning against the bed. "Is he sick? He said he had a sore throat and that he was tired."

"Seems okay to me. I ain't a babysitter."

"Oh, yes, you are." Deb staggered to her feet and marched across the room. "You listen to me. You have my son. You took him, and if anything happens to him, your boss won't get one more thing out of me except a bullet to the head. Now, I'm going to ask you again. Is my son sick?"

The man coughed. "He seems okay. He's tired a lot and started whining about his throat so I gave him some ice cream. Look, you talked to him and now I gotta go. We'll be in touch."

When the man ended the call, Deb threw the phone at the bed. "Bobby didn't sound good."

"Maybe he's just tired and sleeping a lot because he's cooped up with that guy. They're probably not taking him out to play or letting him get any exercise." He walked to the bed and retrieved the phone. Deb needed this thing in working order.

"The important thing is—" he crossed the room and took her hands "—you spoke to him and he's alive."

"You're right. What do you think they've told him?"

He gathered her hands and held them against his chest. "That's another thing. They're not going to be mean to him or freak him out. They want a calm kid on their hands, or at least as calm as they can get him keeping him away from his mother. The ice cream is a good sign. They're trying to make him happy."

She chewed on her bottom lip but left her hands in his. "The sore throat worries me. He had that before…before he was kidnapped. That's why I took him to the doctor."

"Maybe it's just the flu. It's that time of year."

"The sooner I get him home, the better."

"In the meantime, I'm here to take care of his mom, and she needs more than ice cream, too. So let's go out and get dinner like we planned."

"I wish he had told me what they want from

me next. I just want to get through this. I'm tired of his games."

"He'll tell you soon enough. Dinner—we have something to celebrate. You talked to Bobby for the first time since he was taken, proving that Zendaris needs you as much as you need him."

"Okay, dinner, but nothing fancy. I wore my only fancy dress last night, and that didn't go so well."

"Not for Dr. Herndon, but it couldn't have worked out better for you."

Hunching her shoulders, she pulled her hands away from his grasp. "Ugh, I don't like thinking about it that way. Some of his blood spattered on my dress, you know."

"If more than one person wanted Herndon dead, he didn't stand a chance, whether he'd danced with you or not."

"I know you're right." She scooped her hair back from her makeup-free face. "Since I had Bobby, I haven't been doing a lot of the heavy lifting for Prospero. I'm not used to these assignments anymore—the violence, the car chases, the dead bodies. I've been doing more analysis than fieldwork."

"I don't know that you ever get used to someone dropping dead in front of you."

"I'm glad it's not just a *girl* thing."

"Not." He slid his jacket from a hanger in the

closet. "And we are going casual—lobster place outside of town, pick up your own food at the counter, sawdust on the floor."

"That sounds about right."

They took a taxi to the restaurant. Beau didn't think Zendaris was having Deb followed, but that didn't mean they had to drive around in the car he'd provided her.

They joined the long line of customers waiting to place their orders and both picked out a couple of lobsters, some fried clams and coleslaw. They took their bottles of beer to a table and waited for their feasts to be delivered.

Beau had been worried that the call from Bobby would sink Deb into a depression, but she seemed revitalized—ready to take on Zendaris instead of cowering from him.

Beau had finished half his beer by the time their food was delivered to their table.

Deb's eyes widened when the server plopped the plate on the picnic table in front of her. "I may be in over my head here."

"That lobster may look big but you'll have to work to get to all his good parts."

"*Its* good parts." She wrinkled her nose. "Don't refer to it as a he."

Beau laughed and cracked open the first claw. He dug out the succulent meat and drenched it in drawn butter. When he placed it on his tongue, it almost melted. He closed his eyes. "Mmm."

"I think you have it right. Do the hard work first, and then when you're tired out eat the easy stuff."

He helped her crack her lobster, but being Deb, she insisted on taking over and doing it herself. He'd want a wife like that—someone independent, not clingy.

Not that he was thinking about a wife. His gaze shifted to Deb licking melted butter from her fingers. Not even one like this. At least not now. Or maybe ever.

"What?" She covered her face with a greasy paper napkin. "Is that gross?"

"Is what gross?"

"Licking my fingers."

"Not. At. All. You can lick anything you like." He sucked on an empty claw to discourage the wicked grin forming on his face.

She pointed at him with her little sharp fork, a piece of lobster still hanging from the end. "That's Loki right there. That look. You must've had women across the world tossing their panties in the air with that look."

He choked and a quantity of beer fizzed through his nose. "Is that why you think I got into this business?"

"I know that played a role in my Prospero teammate, Gage's, decision."

"Gage Booker, the senator's son?" He took another swig of beer, managing to swallow this one. "That's because he's a suave, smooth-talking SOB."

"And you're…"

"Not."

"Right." She popped a fried clam into her mouth and puckered her lips as she chewed.

Beau never realized eating greasy seafood could be so erotic, although he should've known better. The very first meal they'd shared together had wound up all over their naked bodies.

He tapped his empty beer bottle. "Do you want another? We're taking a taxi home, and I don't think Zendaris is going to contact you tonight."

Her face grew still and she dropped a clam that had been making its way to her mouth back into her plate. "No, I'd better not."

He could've kicked himself for bringing up Zendaris just when she'd seemed to relax a little. "Bobby's okay, Deb. Having another beer is not going to make a difference in how fast we get him back."

"It feels wrong." She crumpled up her napkin and tossed it into the silver bucket brimming with lobster shells.

"I know it does, and I'm not trying to make

you forget about Bobby's predicament, but being a nervous wreck is not going to help him."

"It's a more appropriate response than noshing on lobster and guzzling beer."

"You're not guzzling beer." He leaned forward and dabbed a spot of butter from the corner of her mouth. "Reclaiming your strength and confidence has helped him and will help him. You talked to him for the first time. That had to make him feel better."

"Him and me both, but I think I'll skip the second beer. You go ahead though."

A phone vibrated and Deb jumped. "Is that mine?"

"I think it's mine." Beau felt his pocket, his fingers brushing his buzzing phone. He pulled it out and checked the display. His heart lurched. Jack.

"I'm going to take this call outside. Can you get me another beer?"

Her green eyes glittered in her pale face. "Business?"

"Different business." He lied as smoothly as he would to any quarry he was tracking.

He scuffed through the sawdust on the floor, and pushed through the restaurant's side door to an empty porch. If Jack was calling instead of texting, it had to be important.

"Loki. What's the problem, Jack?"

"You are."

Beau's nostrils flared and his eyes narrowed as he watched Deb through the window pick up a beer at the counter. Looked like he was going to need it.

"What do you mean?"

"Cut the bull, Loki. We know all about you and Deb. You're off the case."

Chapter Ten

Maybe just one sip.

Deb tilted Beau's bottle of beer to her lips. The earthy taste of hops and grains filled her mouth and bubbled against her tongue.

Beau was right. She had to stay strong for Bobby. She couldn't turn into that spineless pile of rags she'd been when she'd first discover d his kidnapping. Her weakness had wasted valuable time and caused missed opportunities.

Who knew how much detail she'd ignored from that first phone call, from the daycare worker's information?

Swiveling her head, she picked out Beau on the side porch of the restaurant. He had his back to the window, but the set of his shoulders and the stiffness of his back screamed out *argument*.

If that was a business call, business wasn't so good.

Suspicion flared in her gut. Those old feelings

and instincts that had vanished the past week were creeping back into her consciousness.

If Beau wanted her to feel empowered, so be it.

She slammed the bottle on the table and pushed to her feet. The soles of her tennis shoes kicked up sawdust on their way to the porch. She eased open the door and held her breath.

She couldn't catch any of Beau's words, but his tone was unmistakable.

She took one step onto the porch, and he spun around, gripping his phone in one hand like a weapon. His ferocity tumbled from him in waves, encompassing her and making her knees tremble. Amid all the talk of families and children and the sexual teasing, she'd almost forgotten who he was.

"Eavesdropping?"

The word hung between them, creating a veil of mistrust on both sides.

"Are you worried about what I might've discovered if I had been?"

He dipped his head and rested his forehead against one end of the phone. "The game's up, Deb."

Her heart fluttered and her knees practically wobbled. Had Zendaris discovered the truth about the murder? "What game?"

"The game I've been playing with Prospero."

Her knees crumpled, but she managed to fold

onto a cold bench. She crossed her arms and tucked her hands under her armpits. "Wh-what does that mean, exactly? Do they know you've been working with me?"

"Not quite. It's not as bad as that."

She scooted further onto the bench before she slipped off and gulped in a few lungfuls of cold air. "Get to the point, Beau."

"Jack found out about us." He smacked the phone against his palm. "Somehow he discovered we'd met before, had spent the night together."

"Okay." She released her breath in small spurts where it formed gusts of fog in the air. "Did he mention how he found out?"

His brows jumped to his hairline. "Why does that matter? He's Jack Coburn, that's how he found out."

It mattered because the only people she'd told about that night were her brothers in arms— Cade, J.D. and Gage. If they'd ratted on her to Jack, it meant they no longer had her back. It meant they believed the worst of her.

"It doesn't." She shook her head and drew her hand across her mouth. "What's the upshot? Why were you arguing with Jack?"

"Did you hear any of that?"

"Just the tone of your voice, your stance, the way you turned on me when you heard my approach."

"Sorry." He ran a hand through his hair. "He's taking me off the case, Deb."

"He told you that?"

"When Dr. Herndon was murdered, he figured there had to be some connection between his death and you and Zendaris. He wondered why I hadn't made the connection, and then he found out about our connection."

"Does he know you're helping me?"

"I don't think so. If he suspects it, he didn't accuse me of it. If he believes you turned, he'd have to believe it of me, too."

"What next, Beau?" She shoved her hands beneath her bouncing legs, not wanting to hear his answer.

"He's putting someone else on the job."

She jumped up and stalked to the end of the porch and then swung around. "That's just great. I have Zendaris yanking my strings like a puppet master, some shadow spy after the same thing I'm after, and now some hired spook coming after me—one I didn't happen to share a hot night with. And Bobby's still being held captive."

If she hadn't just vowed to man-up and start acting like a Prospero agent, she'd cry.

"And me."

"Huh?" That's the only word she could manage to squeeze past her tight throat.

He hooked his thumbs in the belt loops of his jeans and drew back his shoulders. "You have me."

Those were the sweetest three words she'd heard all night. She threw herself against his chest and wrapped her arms around his waist. "You don't know how good that makes me feel."

He stroked her hair, and just like that she didn't feel like crying anymore. They'd formed a team, and with their combined experiences and resources, they'd be unbeatable.

She lifted her cheek from his chest and parked her head beneath his chin. "You don't think Jack would send one of my Team Three members after me, do you?"

"No way." Cupping her jaw, he tilted up her head. "He knows how strong that bond is. He knows their first loyalty is to you."

"But not if I broke that trust. That's what he thinks, isn't it? Maybe that's what they think, too."

"Is that what you'd believe of them?" He traced her outer ear with the pad of his thumb. "Would you naturally assume one of your team members had gone to the other side just because your boss told you he had?"

Pressing her lips together, she shook her head from side to side. "No. I'd never believe that of any of them."

"And I'm sure they feel the same way about

you. I may be an independent contractor now, a lone wolf, but I experienced that same bond when I was active duty. Jack Coburn is not going to send one of your own after you."

"Then we're safe."

"Don't be too confident. There are some good people out there, and Jack knows all of them. I found you, and it wasn't hard."

One of her shoulders rose and fell. "You're Loki."

"Yeah, well, Loki may have just ruined his reputation." He hung an arm around her shoulder and nudged her toward the door and light and people and warmth.

"I'm sorry."

"Don't be. Jack was right—any gun for hire who could be deterred by a pretty face and a one-night stand might want to look into retirement."

"Jack said that?"

"Something like it. You know Jack—a man of few words."

The warm room sucked them in, and they wandered back to their table hand in hand. "I'm going to have another beer after all."

"Why not celebrate? The charade is up and I don't have to go on lying to Prospero. I hate lying to my friends, anyway."

Deb dropped her lashes over her eyes and reached for Beau's bottle of warm beer. "Do you want a fresh one?"

"Absolutely, but let me get them this time."

He rose from the table and sauntered to the counter, way too relaxed for a man who'd just been fired.

She hated lying, too. She had to find a way to tell Beau he was Bobby's father. She'd have to wait until she had Bobby safely home and in her arms though. Beau's worry for Bobby stemmed from his concern for all children and maybe, just maybe, his feelings for her. If she told him about Bobby before they rescued him, his emotions would cloud the mission.

He'd be even more worried about Bobby if he knew he was his own...wouldn't he? At the very least Beau's anger toward her and her deception might compromise the entire plan.

She'd wait.

He returned, carrying two sweating bottles. "They replaced my warm beer for free. We've gotta come back here when this is all over."

She smiled while she took a sip of her beer. She wanted nothing more than to come back and eat lobsters with Beau and Bobby as a family. But Beau didn't want a family.

And he hated liars.

THE NEXT MORNING, Deb woke up heavy-eyed. Beau had gone to the gym early, letting her sleep in. She had to make up for the sleep she'd missed during the night. The sleep she'd missed tossing and turning and being tuned in to every little movement from the bed next to hers.

Several times, she'd imagined that Beau was leaving his bed for hers. She'd lie still and wait for his touch, wait for his masculine scent to wash over her, wait for his whispered words of want and need.

She'd waited all night long.

By the time morning rolled in, her muscles ached, she could barely move her stiff neck and a foul mood hovered over her like a miasma.

Beau had seen the writing on the wall almost immediately and taken off for the gym, telling her to get some more sleep.

The extra hours of sleep hadn't done much for her sore muscles and stiff neck, which she attributed to her workout yesterday. But sleep had softened her mood.

She had nobody to blame but herself that Beau hadn't made any moves on her. She'd made it clear the first night he'd tracked her down that her worry and desperation as a mother had shut down the spigot of sexual need and desire.

What had changed?

Every time she fantasized about Beau, black clouds of guilt would rush in on the heels of the fantasy. She'd mentally berate herself for thinking about her own desires while her little boy was being held hostage somewhere.

But it was more than sex she craved from Beau. She longed for that human connection that had been missing from her life for so long. She thirsted for the comfort and completeness of making love with a man, especially this man, the father of her beloved child.

To form that bond with Beau again would be to complete the circle of their family. She'd begun to feel as if there were some mystical power in making that connection, as if that family bond could clear a path to finding and rescuing Bobby.

Beau's laptop beeped in the corner. She eyed it but decided against mucking around with his databases and search engines.

She yawned and stretched. She could use some juice and coffee but after the lobster and fried clams and beers last night, she couldn't face another morsel of food.

Deb rolled out of bed and stumbled into the shower. The warm water and fragrant steam did nothing to wake her up, so she twisted the dial in the other direction. As the cool water hit her back, her teeth chattered and sent a wave of goose bumps across her body. That's what she needed.

She dressed in the same old jeans but swapped the T-shirt she'd worn yesterday for a fresh one.

If Zendaris kept her on the line much longer, she'd need to hit the mall again.

The door clicked and Beau poked his head into the room. "Is everyone decent?"

"If you can call these dirty jeans and T-shirt decent, then I guess I qualify."

He placed a cup of coffee on the table and held up a paper bag. "I figured you'd sleep through breakfast, so I picked up a coffee and a couple of scones for you."

"Thanks." She waved her toothbrush at his laptop. "Your computer beeped while you were gone, but I didn't want to mess up anything."

"Maybe my sources found something on our guy." He pulled a scone from the bag and bit off the corner.

"I thought those were for me." She took in his damp T-shirt clinging to his chest and the sweatshirt he'd thrown over the back of the chair. "Where have you been anyway? Since when does the hotel gym have scones and coffee?"

"I took a run along the river. I couldn't take the treadmill in the gym—too boring."

"No suspicious activity out there? No one lurking around the hotel?"

"Do you think my replacement is going to find

you that fast?" He brushed the crumbs from the table into his palm.

"I don't think your replacement is going to find me at all." She joined him at the table, where he'd pressed a few keys on the laptop, and took a sip of her coffee. "Now that you're a disgraced spy, is someone going to bust you for accessing top secret databases?"

"How fast do you think Jack works? He just fired me last night. I doubt if the entire intelligence community knows." He rubbed his hands together as lines of data scrolled down the screen. "I'm not persona non grata yet."

He pulled up a chair and nodded to the other one. "Have a seat and start eating that other scone before I demolish that one, too."

She sat down next to him and plunged her fingers into the white bag. She broke off a piece of the crumbly scone and popped it into her mouth. "Can you make anything out of all that?"

Beau was running his finger down the monitor, stopping occasionally to jab at a piece of information as if prodding it to give him more.

"Look at this guy, Deb." He scrolled up the screen to one of the pictures they'd matched before. "He's known as Damon. He's a South American, has been involved with the drug cartels down there. He dropped off the radar a few years ago, but still has his contacts so he's not out of the game. But which game?"

"No more drugs?" She stared into the dark beady eyes of the man, hoping for some recognition.

"He hasn't been connected to the drug trade for a few years. Maybe he switched to weapons. His drug connections would be handy for Zendaris."

"Specialties?"

"Weapons. Surveillance. He's also the muscle."

"He has enough of them." She bit off another piece of scone and covered her mouth when she talked. "If he's our man, it would be great to have at least one face to pick out in a crowd."

"Exactly. I know I could recognize him again. Who knows where he'd take us if we followed him?"

"He could take us to Bobby."

"And that's the kind of break we need."

"Any of the others on our short list look good?" She swirled her coffee in the cup before taking another sip.

"Not as good as this guy."

Crumpling the pastry bag in one hand, Deb rose from the table and tossed the bag in the trash can. She flipped through the free paper the hotel delivered, but Dr. Herndon's death didn't warrant a place on the national news scene for the second day running.

"Have you heard anything more about the investigation into Herndon's death?"

"Nothing. I guess they're waiting for the autopsy report."

"And nothing more about the mysterious black-haired seductress?"

"Nope, and since Herndon was single the media isn't crawling all over that angle."

"What angle is Jack taking? Does he think I'm responsible?"

"Involved? Yes. Responsible? Jury is still out on that one."

She carefully refolded the paper along its crease. "What did you say to Jack last night? Why were you arguing with him?"

"He'd just fired me. I was trying my best to talk him out of it." He kicked his long legs up on the chair she'd just vacated. "I admitted that we'd hooked up years ago but insisted it meant nothing and the news that I'd be tracking you barely registered as a blip on my radar."

"Ouch. Did he believe you?"

"Whether he believed me or not never came up. Fact is, I withheld information from him. You don't withhold information from Jack Coburn."

"I know." She dropped on the bed. "Look where it got me."

"Are you sure your best bet all along wasn't to tell Prospero that Zendaris had kidnapped your son?"

"No." She stuffed her feet into her tennis shoes. "When someone has your child, your first instinct is to do exactly what they tell you to do."

"I get that, but it's not like your team members would jeopardize the safety of your son. They wouldn't have come in with guns blazing."

"I just had a feeling that Zendaris would know if I went to Prospero. I don't know how or why, but that feeling controlled every move I made after Bobby's kidnapping."

"He knew enough about your life to have someone pretend to be Robert. I can't tell you if it was a good move or a bad one to keep Prospero in the dark. You bought yourself some security but opened up some difficulties for yourself. Did you really think your boss wouldn't notice that you'd dropped out of sight?"

She sighed. "I took a leave of absence. I thought that would be good enough."

"Well, here we are."

"Yep." She tied her shoes and stomped on the carpet.

"Going somewhere? Mind if I tag along?"

She crossed her arms and tilted her head. "Because you want to or because you think I need protection?"

"Does it matter?" He stripped off his T-shirt

and dug through the dresser drawer where he'd dumped his purchases. He pulled out a clean T-shirt and the jeans he'd worn over the past few days. "Can you wait while I hop in the shower? I won't be long."

"I'll wait for you." Her gaze lingered on the wedges of muscle shifting across his chest and shoulders. Could she wait for him while he decided whether or not he wanted to be a father to Bobby?

She'd have to tell him first.

While Beau showered, Deb flipped through the TV channels. Had the untimely death of a scientist already slipped off the news radar? She should be thankful. She didn't need to have her picture flashed on the news again, although it added credibility to her actions for Zendaris.

And Prospero.

Had her Team Three cohorts recognized her from the grainy photo?

Beau had finished his shower faster than she thought humanly possible. He burst through the bathroom door, fully dressed and toweling his short hair.

At least he was sparing her the sight of his half-clothed body for once. She couldn't take much more temptation.

"Are you ready?" He rubbed a little gel between his palms and slicked it over his wet hair.

"Are you?" She made a circle with her index

finger in his general direction. "I didn't realize Loki used so much hair product."

He held up the tube. "This? Just keeps things in order."

"Got it." She held up her hands.

"Where are we going?"

"I thought I'd take the T into Boston and follow that red line painted on the sidewalk that goes past all the historical sites. I've done it before. It takes you from Boston Common all the way to the *USS Constitution* in Boston Harbor."

"Sounds like an all-day adventure."

"What else do we have to do except wait around for Zendaris's instructions—and he seems to be taking his sweet time."

"You're right, and it'll take your mind off… things."

"My mind's never off Bobby, if that's what you mean." Deb zipped up her jacket and pressed her lips together just in case Beau thought a smile meant she'd forgotten about her son…their son.

"Hey." He pulled her toward him by the edges of her jacket and yanked her zipper up to her chin. "I know that. You don't have to prove anything. You wouldn't be contemplating murder and mayhem at Zendaris's behest if Bobby didn't mean the world to you."

"It's just that sometimes…" Her lip trembled and she bit it.

He wrapped his arms around her and held her

flush against his body. His heart beat strong and sure beneath her cheek and she closed her eyes to soak in his strength.

She allowed herself one minute of weakness, and then she pushed away from him. "Okay, let's get reacquainted with the Revolution."

They picked up a pamphlet in the Common and followed the red line painted on the sidewalk. When they hit Faneuil Hall, Deb's stomach grumbled, reminding her of the paltry breakfast she'd consumed in the hotel room—and Beau had stolen half of that.

Beau pointed to the food court. "I'm pretty sure that wasn't around in 1776, but I'm glad it is now."

"You must've been reading my mind—or listening to my stomach. I'm starving."

"I'm up for a burger and fries, you?"

"I'm going to the pizza place." She jerked her thumb toward a counter with a red-and-green-striped awning.

"Meet you back at a table in this general area. Do you have money?"

"It's on Zendaris." She waved a twenty at him.

Deb ordered a couple of slices of thin-crust pepperoni pizza, a small salad and a diet soda. Bobby had just been discovering the joys of pizza before he'd lost his appetite. A gnawing sense of worry joined the hunger pangs in her belly. She hoped Bobby's jailer was feeding him more than ice cream.

She dipped her hand into a canister, grabbed a few packets of Italian dressing and tossed them onto her plastic tray. She maneuvered through a tour group set free for lunch and claimed a table in the middle of everything.

A few minutes later Beau turned from the counter of the burger place, peering over two plates of food.

Deb waved and he weaved his way through the tables to join her, and plunked his plates onto the table.

She snatched a fry from the towering stack. "That's for eating my scone this morning."

He shoved the plate toward her. "You can have a lot more than that if you want."

"I'm good." She swallowed the fry and picked up her pizza. "How do you like the tour?"

"It's interesting. Those men who signed the Declaration risked a lot, didn't they?"

"Nothing worth having comes without some element of risk."

"I agree." He nodded and bit into his burger.

She dabbed her lips with a napkin and took a sip of her soda. She'd do well to remember that. If she wanted Bobby to know his father, she'd have to risk Beau's wrath and tell him about his son.

They ate their lunches, talking about the tour

and history and their favorite players in the Revolution. They talked about everything but Zendaris and Prospero and the anti-drone plans.

They even talked about Bobby. Deb peppered her conversation with stories about him and how he'd changed her life. This had to be gradual. Once she sprung Beau's paternity on him, he had to have a feel for Bobby. She didn't want Bobby to be a complete stranger to his father.

Beau flipped open the brochure on the walking tour. "Are you up for the rest of the walk? Paul Revere's house and the *USS Constitution* and Bunker Hill?"

"Let's do it." She collected her trash and piled it on the tray. "We may not be here tomorrow."

They dumped their trash in the cans and stacked their trays on top. They went out a side door to continue their walk.

A light changed and Deb stepped off the curb. Out of the corner of her eye, she saw a car surge past the rest.

As she turned to face it, her world slowed down. The large black SUV careened through the intersection, heading straight toward her. Beau yelled out. Deb took one step and froze. Would she be continuing into the path of the car? Should she jump back?

Then she realized it wouldn't matter. Where she went, the SUV would follow.

Chapter Eleven

The SUV bore down on them, narrowly missing a car scooting through the intersection. Beau called out to Deb, but she seemed frozen, transfixed by the black vehicle.

If she didn't move within a split second, he'd have to move her.

Hell, what was he waiting for? He hooked an arm around her waist and yanked her back onto the sidewalk, smashing her into the corner of a building.

She gasped and it sounded as if she'd spent all her breath. A woman screamed—not Deb. Tires squealed, filling the air with the smell of burning rubber.

When Beau looked up, the SUV was speeding around the next corner. Someone had covered the license plate with paper.

Of course.

A woman hovered above them, panting and cursing. "Can you believe that idiot? He almost took us out."

Wouldn't be the first time.

"Are you okay, ma'am?"

"I'm all right, just shaking like a damned leaf. Is your wife okay? That moron came closer to her than me."

Deb raised her head, her eyes wide in a white face. "Oh, my God, he almost hit us. Was anyone hurt?"

The woman pressed a hand to her forehead. "No, but it wasn't for lack of effort on that driver's part. He went right through the light and then it seemed as if he waited for pedestrians to enter the crosswalk before stepping on the gas."

Deb had sat up and was leaning against the building. A slight scrape marred her smooth cheek. "Thank God he didn't hit anyone. Did anyone get his license plate?"

"Big black behemoth—that's all I saw." She shrugged, straightened her jacket and stepped into the crosswalk again.

"Beau?"

"Big black behemoth with paper covering the plates."

Deb covered her mouth. "Then it was deliberate, and I don't think it was aimed at Miss Pink Jacket."

"I doubt it."

"What if it *is* Zendaris?"

"Deb—" he hooked an arm beneath hers "—we're not going to discuss this on the street."

She brushed off her jeans. "Let's continue this walk."

"Are you crazy?"

"What? Do you think he's going to try it again?"

"Stay close to me."

"So he can take both of us out?"

"I thought you were convinced he wasn't going to try the same stunt twice?"

"He's not, unless he has another blind car waiting in the wings."

They continued their walk, but this time, Beau kept his arm firmly around Deb's shoulders. When she squirmed under the weight of his arm, he took her hand and pulled her close, matching her step for long step.

"Why would you think Zendaris was trying to kill you when he's using you to go after the anti-drone plans?"

"Is he? Is that what he's using me for? So far he's had me rob a jewelry store and kill a man. How is that bringing him any closer to the plans or me any closer to Bobby?"

"What do you think he's doing?"

"Playing some sadistic game. He can't get to Cade, J.D. or Gage, so he's taking all his fury out on me."

"I have a different take on it." He pulled her

onto a bench looking out on a park with brown, wintry grass. "I think someone else is after the plans, knows you're after the same thing and doesn't want to lose out to you. He's trying to eliminate the competition."

"Who's he working for?"

Beau rested his ankle on his knee. "Maybe he's someone like me—a freelancer."

"Maybe he's working for Prospero."

"I was working for Prospero when the first shot was attempted in the hotel room."

Turning toward him, she placed her hands on his thigh. "Jack Coburn has excellent instincts. Maybe he knew from the get-go you weren't to be trusted."

"Thanks."

"Maybe he was testing you."

"Seems kind of convoluted to me."

"If your scenario is correct, Beau, we can't let this other guy beat us to the punch." She dug her nails into his leg. "If he gets the plans before I do, it's over for Bobby."

"Don't think like that." He lightly rapped his knuckles on her head. "We're double the trouble. Nobody is going to beat us at our own game."

She managed a weak smile. "Onto the *USS Constitution?*"

"For liberty and justice for all."

"That's the Pledge, not the Constitution."

"Conceived in liberty and dedicated to justice?"

"Gettysburg Address."

"I give up." He stood up and pulled her to her feet. "I obviously need the rest of this history lesson."

When they got back to the hotel, Beau stopped at the sundry shop and bought some cotton balls and antiseptic spray. In the room, he dabbed the scratch on her face, and she sucked in a breath.

After Beau treated her scratch, Deb hopped onto the bed and punched the pillows behind her. "If the guy in the SUV today is the same one with the high-powered rifle at the other hotel, he must be following us. That's just one of many things that scares me right now. If he's tracking us, who's to say Zendaris isn't tracking me. And if he is, he knows about you."

"Whoa, you're making a lot of leaps here."

Tilting her head back, she closed her eyes. "I just want Bobby back. I don't care about the plans, Zendaris or even Prospero. I just want to hold my son in my arms."

The mattress sank and Deb fluttered her lashes. Beau was on the edge of the bed, his blue eyes brimming with some emotion she couldn't identify.

Was it pity? She'd take that. She'd take anything from him at this point. Once she told him about Bobby, she may never get another chance to be with him.

And she wanted to be with him.

Beau inched closer. "Turn around."

Folding her legs beneath her, she presented her back to him. His strong hands closed around her neck.

"You've been on a roller coaster for over a week."

With his thumbs, he rubbed circles at the base of her neck.

"It's been more bearable since you showed up." She dropped her chin to her chest.

"This is not something you want to face on your own." His knuckles massaged the sides of her neck. "Even if you're a tough-as-nails Prospero agent."

She huffed out a breath. "Is that what you think?"

"That's what I know. That's the woman I was attracted to in Zurich, and I've seen flashes of her in Boston—fearless, determined."

"I told you, I changed after Bobby."

"And I like this Deb even more. You're still fearless and determined—this time to protect your son—but you have some soft edges now that you were missing before."

His hands moved to her back, smoothing over the sharp angles of her shoulder blades.

"That's what having kids will do to you." She rolled her head back and hissed through her teeth when he dug his fingers into the flesh on either side of her spine.

"Does that hurt?"

"In a totally good way."

"You have so many knots in your neck, shoulders and back. You're holding all your tension in those areas."

"Are you a masseuse in your spare time?"

He chuckled in her ear, a low sound that made her mouth water.

"One of my sisters is a masseuse. She's taught me a thing or two. She claims every time I come back to the family homestead, I'm tied up in knots."

"That doesn't surprise me. You always seem coiled and ready to spring."

He lifted her hair and pressed his lips against the back of her neck. "Not always."

If she melted against him right now would he take the hint? "Beau…"

"Shh." He gathered her hair in his hands and buried his face in it. "If you don't want more, that's okay. If you do, that's okay, too. I'm not going to think you're less of a mother or less of an agent if you want to make love with me. It is what it is, Deb."

She turned toward him, and her hair slipped from his hands, falling around her shoulders. "I can't pretend anymore. I can't pretend that you're just some man who turned from a predator to a protector. You're a man who's been on my mind for the past three years."

"God, I'm glad to hear you say that." He encircled her waist with his hands. "I thought it was just me. I thought I'd built up a night of incredible sex into some epic encounter that I'd never experience again."

Stroking her hands across his shoulders, she smiled. "An epic adventure—yeah, it did feel like that."

She couldn't resist those lips a second longer. She shifted forward, and he took it from there.

When their lips met, a jolt of pure desire zapped her from head to toe. He felt it, too, because he held her tighter as if he was afraid she'd fall from the bed.

His hands tangled in her hair as he positioned her head, angling his mouth across hers. Their tongues tangled. Their breaths came heavy and hard.

Would it be like the first time they'd collided? Frantic. Eager. Breathless.

No. Tonight Beau Slater held her in his arms,

not Loki. Tonight the father of her child held her in his arms.

He deepened the kiss, and stroked her back, slow and easy. Had he read her mind? This time the reckless abandon that had possessed them three years ago had morphed into a slow sensual dance.

Sitting back, he slipped his hands beneath her legs and pulled them straight, causing her to slide onto her back. He rolled up the hem of her T-shirt and trailed rough fingertips across her belly.

"This time I want to fully appreciate every inch of you." He nudged the shirt up farther and ran his thumbs across the bottom crescents of her breasts through her lacy bra.

She gazed at him through her lashes. "Are you going to take ten minutes to get my T-shirt off?"

In one swift movement, he yanked it up and over her head. Then he placed it over her eyes. "Maybe you need to stop directing the action here, lie back and enjoy."

"I can do that."

The makeshift blindfold made every touch and every sensation a surprise, a welcome surprise. When she thought he'd continue his exploration of her breasts, he tickled the lobe of her ear with his tongue instead. When she thought he'd follow that up with a kiss to her mouth, he slid his hand beneath her bra and cupped her breast while teasing her nipple.

And on it went. Blindfolded, she became a canvas for his fingers, mouth, lips and tongue—and she still had on the majority of her clothing.

Finally, he slid her jeans over her hips and pulled them off, along with her panties. He brushed his hands along her inner thighs, parting her legs.

She held her breath, as tingles raced along her flesh, gathering in all the sensitive areas of her body. She could feel the heat emanating from his skin and knew all the rustling and clinking had come from the removal of his own clothing.

She almost snatched the blindfold from her eyes so she could feast on the sight of his naked form, but then she'd spoil his party.

He straddled her and the tight flesh of his erection brushed her belly.

Unbidden, her hips rose from the bed in anticipation.

Beau clicked his tongue. "Impatient woman."

Then he flicked her nipple with the tip of his tongue.

She gasped and began to draw her legs together, but he caught the insides of her thighs with both hands. "Keep your legs open—for me."

The growl in his voice had her quivering like

a bowl of Jell-O, but she obeyed his command. Did she have a choice?

He continued toying with her nipples—tongue and fingers, pleasure and pain. His game had her squirming on the mattress beneath him.

After tweaking it, he sucked one nipple between his lips. As he pulled the aching nipple into his mouth, one finger drew a hard line from her navel to her throbbing folds.

The shock thrust her pelvis upward, and a groan escaped from her lips. "Why are you torturing me?"

He nipped her lower lip with his teeth. "Do you want me to stop?"

Raising her hands, she dug her fingernails into the first flesh they met—one hip and one arm. "Don't you dare. But can't you lift the blindfold so I can see where the next sneak attack is going to land?"

"And why would I do that?" The bed dipped on either side of her and she felt his knees at her hips.

Again, she hitched up her hips, but he cupped her breasts and squeezed them together. The hot flesh of his erection eased between the cleft of her breasts, poking her chin.

Two could play at this game.

She dropped her chin to her chest and stuck out her tongue to sweep it across his smooth skin.

He groaned but didn't stop. Neither did she. After a few more strokes, the time he spent close to her mouth increased until he stopped pumping her breasts altogether.

Hitching up on her elbows, she took him fully into her mouth. When she reached for the blindfold, he cinched her wrists.

"Not yet. I'm not done with you yet."

She gave a throaty laugh. "I thought I was just about to finish *you* off."

"You've clearly forgotten this is Loki you're dealing with—master of self-control."

He slid down her body and plunged his tongue into the warm folds between her legs. He drove her to the edge of madness with his mouth, lips and tongue.

As her belly coiled and her muscles tensed, he pulled away from her. She cried out and then amplified that cry when he drove into her.

He pulled the T-shirt from her face and scorched her with a gaze of blue fire.

She exploded around him. Wave after wave of pleasure surged through her body, and she clamped her legs around his hips to ride out the storm.

He gave a great shudder, slammed against her

once, held his position for a few seconds and then continued stroke after stroke as he emptied his seed deep inside her.

When he finished he collapsed to the side of her, nuzzling her neck and caressing her breasts. "Can I just say, Madam Spy, that you're the best lay I've ever had in my life?"

"Aww, I'll bet you say that to all the lady spies." She punched him in the shoulder where her fist met solid muscle.

He grabbed her hand and kissed every knuckle. "No, I don't."

"Food, blindfolds, you're quite the inventive lover."

"I think the food was your idea."

"You started it by putting that strawberry in my... Never mind."

He had moved from her knuckles to her fingertips, kissing each one. "If I was so inventive, why'd you run back to the other guy so fast?"

Her heart skidded to a virtual stop in her chest. She did not want to have this conversation about Bobby's father. Not yet.

She smoothed her hand across the hair sprinkled across his chest. "You were Loki. You never even told me your real name."

"You never asked."

The cell phone, which was never far out of her

reach, buzzed, and a breath hitched in her throat. "It's him."

Beau reached across her body and picked up the phone. He held it out to her and she grabbed it.

"Yes?"

Zendaris snarled over the phone. "Are you playing me for a fool?"

Chapter Twelve

The rosy afterglow on Deb's cheeks faded to white. Beau's heart slammed against his rib cage. Deb hadn't put the phone on speaker and being out of the loop even for a second had his blood pressure going through the roof.

"Wh-what are you talking about?"

Beau poked her thigh to get her attention. She twisted her head around and her eyes widened as if she'd forgotten his existence. She blinked a few times and pressed the speaker button.

"You told Prospero, didn't you?"

Deb choked and Beau cursed under his breath.

"I did not tell Prospero. Why would you think that? Do you really believe I'd kill an innocent man and turn around and tell Prospero about it?"

"Who said Dr. Herndon was an innocent man?"

"What are you suggesting?"

"I'm suggesting you called someone in for help."

Deb hunched her shoulders, and he tucked

the sheet around her waist. Had Zendaris spotted him?

"I didn't call anyone in for help, least of all Prospero. The word on the street is I'm a traitor and Prospero doesn't suffer traitors kindly."

"Someone is shadowing you, shadowing me. I don't like it."

"Did you think a Prospero agent could turn and nobody would notice?" Her sharp tone filled Beau with admiration. This Deb Sinclair was finished with cowering and shaking at Zendaris's every command.

That's it, Deb. A good defense is a good offense.

Her attitude had thrown Zendaris off balance. He paused, and she jumped into the pause.

"If Prospero sent someone after me, it's not another Prospero agent. Coburn doesn't use his agents like that. If someone is on my tail, it's a hired gun." She formed a gun with her fingers and aimed at Beau.

"He'd better not get in the way of my plan. If he does, there will be— How do you Americans say it? A world of hurt…for everybody."

"There's not going to be any world of hurt. What are your plans? What do you want me to do next?"

"Break into Dr. Herndon's house and get the anti-drone plans."

Deb's mouth dropped open, but Beau didn't know why she was so surprised. They'd figured Zendaris had those plans in his sights.

She recovered quickly. "Where's his house and is anyone watching it?"

"His house is outside of Boston, and whether or not anyone is watching the house is your problem, not mine." He gave her the directions to Herndon's house, which Deb scribbled on the hotel notepad on the nightstand.

She held the pen poised over the paper. "Where will I find the plans?"

"Again, your problem, Agent Sinclair, not mine." Deb closed her eyes and rolled her lips inward as if to rein in her emotions.

If Zendaris had dared talk to him like that, he'd ram the phone down his throat over the line. But then he didn't have a son to worry about.

"And when I secure the plans, we talk again to discuss the trade."

"If someone doesn't beat you to it."

Deb set her jaw. "Nobody is going to beat me to it. The trade?"

"I'm a man of my word." He coughed. "I think your son's...ah, babysitter...is getting tired of the job anyway."

"Oh?" Deb's eyes flew to Beau's face as she dropped the pen to the floor. "Why is that?"

"Your son hasn't been feeling well."

Was Zendaris telling her this news to keep her off balance? To instill urgency?

"What's wrong with him?" Grabbing a pillow, she hugged it to her chest.

She should've grabbed him instead. Beau slipped a blanket over her shoulders, his arm lingering behind her back—just in case she needed something to lean on.

"I'm sure it's nothing, but you're a mother and you'd want to know. I have a soft spot for mothers, Deb." He paused. "My daughter didn't even have the chance to know her mother."

"I'm sorry—" Beau tugged on the end of her hair "—for your daughter. Every child deserves his or her parents, both of them. What are Bobby's symptoms?"

"I'm not a doctor, and you just killed one so get to his house and get me those plans, or your son is not going to have to worry about his symptoms."

Zendaris ended the call and Deb looked like someone had just punched her in the gut. Zendaris had lured her in with his talk of mothers and his sob story about his wife, whose death was at his door, and then delivered his last words with a hammer.

Deb's hands looked frozen on the phone, so Beau pried it from her fingers and gathered her in his arms like he'd wanted to do five minutes ago. He ran a hand down her stiff back. "It's okay. You can let go now."

Her body melted against his as a sob racked her frame. "He means it, Beau. He'll kill Bobby if I don't deliver those plans. What am I going to do? We've worked so hard to keep those plans out of his hands, but I have to save my son."

"We're going to do both, Deb. We have to do both."

"Bobby's still sick." She covered her face with her hands. "He must feel so abandoned by me right now. He's not feeling well and Mommy isn't there for him. How is he ever going to recover from this?"

He grasped her wrists and pulled her hands from her face. Then he brushed his palms across her wet cheeks. "This experience is not going to scar him for life."

"It took me a long time to get over my abandonment issues. It took a father figure like Robert. A boy needs his father."

Beau swallowed. Did this mean she had plans to go back to Bobby's father when this was all over?

"You'd had a child's life of abandonment, Deb. This is two weeks out of Bobby's life. He's not going to remember. Once he feels his mother's arms around him again, he'll forget you ever left."

"I hope you're right." A shudder ran through her body. She plucked a tissue from the box on the bedside table and dabbed her nose. "I'll bet your mom never left your side when you were sick, did she?"

"My mom?" After the drama of the phone call, he began to notice the cool air on his bare skin so he burrowed back under the covers and pulled Deb along with him. "God, no. My mother was a stay-at-home mom when we were little and when we were sick, she'd hover over us with homemade chicken soup and mentholated rub and disgusting concoctions for sore throats like apple cider vinegar."

She snuggled closer to him and curled her toes against his shins. "But you loved it, didn't you?"

"*Love* isn't the word I'd settle on. Let's just say none of us stayed sick for long."

"You're just saying that." She rubbed his chest with the heel of her hand. "You felt her love right there and you've been able to carry it with you everywhere. That's the kind of love I want to give Bobby."

"And you're giving it to him. You're risking everything to keep him safe, and he feels it—" he tapped the left side of her chest "—right here."

"Do you really think so?"

"There are different types of motherly love, and different types of mothers. How cool is it going to be for Bobby to discover someday that his mom is a kick-ass spy who battled an international arms dealer to keep him safe? I'd say that beats out homemade chicken soup any day."

She turned her head and kissed his arm. "What an amazing thing to say. How did I ever think you were cool and aloof?"

"That's the image I cultivated." He tousled her long hair, which already resembled a red-hued bird's nest. "Of course, if Coburn spreads the word that I took an assignment to protect a woman, there goes my image."

Her long eyelashes drifted closed and fluttered over her eyes. "Mmm, I don't know about that. The ladies will be throwing their panties at you even more than usual."

"The ladies do not throw their panties at me."

Her lips curved into a smile against his chest, and he lightly pinched her bottom. That made her squirm against him, so he did it again, but her breathing had deepened and her lips parted in a long sigh.

He whispered into her ear, "The only panties I want are yours."

THE FOLLOWING DAY, Deb dug into a piece of French toast with a swirl of cinnamon and warm pecans on top. "I can't believe we forgot to eat dinner last night."

"Really?" Beau speared a potato on his plate and dragged it through some sticky egg yolk. "Because it seems to me that you'd skip dinner and every other meal if my stomach didn't remind us to eat."

"It's the nerves. I can't eat when I'm stressed."

He raised one eyebrow as she smothered her French toast with syrup and flagged down the waitress for another side of bacon. "You're obviously not stressed."

"I don't know what it is. I feel energized today." She *did* know the reason. Part of it included Beau's pep talk last night. He thought she was a good mom and that cut loose a heavy burden she'd been carrying on her back like a Sisyphean-sized bolder.

Maybe he'd be more willing to sign up for fatherhood once she told him about Bobby's parentage if he believed she was a good mother. And she planned to tell him just as soon as this nightmare ended.

"It probably has to do with the fact that we're in the homestretch here. You have your final orders from Zendaris, and we're close to ending this."

She held up her hands, crossing her fingers. "I hope so. Were you able to access the floor layout to Herndon's house on the laptop before we came down here?"

"I was, and we're in luck. The house is not that big."

"Maybe that's why he went to the dark side. He wants a bigger home and all the stuff that goes with it. Because if he has those anti-drone plans, he definitely crossed over to the dark side."

"It probably also has to do with his taste in fancy women."

"Tastes like that can get you killed." Deb drew a line through her syrup with the tines of her fork.

"He found that out the hard way—not that the mysterious black-haired beauty at the charity ball had anything to do with his death."

"Do you think that's how Zendaris decided to use me once he got his hands on Bobby? He knew Dr. Herndon's proclivities?"

"He would've formulated a different plan if it had been Cade Stark's son he kidnapped."

"It wasn't Cade's son. He was able to keep his son safe."

"By eventually going to Europe. Aren't his wife and child still there?"

She plucked a pecan from her French toast and sucked it into her mouth. "You are good. That information is supposed to be top secret."

"So is the layout of Dr. Herndon's house, but I managed to get a source to send it to me."

"After breakfast we go up to the room and hash out a plan for entry?"

"For entry and search. The plans could be anywhere in the house. What format do you think they're in?"

"They were in a computer file, but I doubt Herndon left them on his computer. A skilled hacker can get into any computer, which Prospero found out when we first had the plans."

He waved the waitress over for more coffee. "They could be on a thumb drive or a CD, or he could've just printed them out. Will you know what they look like?"

"Oh, yeah." She bit into her last piece of bacon with a crunch and offered the rest to Beau, who took it. "When Cade first stole the plans from Zendaris, we were all briefed on what they contained, if not the particulars. That's why I think Zendaris is using me to do his dirty work instead of one of his usual goons—that and his thirst for revenge."

Beau leaned back in his chair and crossed his arms over his impressive chest. "Don't let him pull at your heartstrings over his dead wife, Deb. Men like Zendaris aren't sentimental. They may think they love their wives and children, but they put them in harm's way every day of their lives. A dude like that would sacrifice Granny if it meant more power and money."

"You're right. All the men on my team recognized that immediately. I was the only one who felt a modicum of guilt over the fact that his wife had been killed in our raid of his factory."

"That's because you have a soft heart." He reached out and dislodged a strand of hair stuck to her cheek.

She snorted. "Nobody has ever accused me of that before, including the girls at the reform school that I busted out of."

"Tough girl." A smile hovered on his sensuous lips.

"Are you making fun of me?"

"Not at all." He held out his hands. "You might kick me where it counts."

"I'd *never* do that." The thought of doing damage to any of Beau's beautiful parts caused her to cringe.

"There's a soft side to Deb Sinclair, and obviously Robert Elder saw that."

Her nose tingled. "Robert had to sandpaper away a bunch of layers to find it, and the process wasn't always pretty. He was a marine, so he was into that tough love."

Beau hunched forward, cupping his mouth with one hand. "So am I. In addition to the blindfold, I have some furry handcuffs."

She kicked his foot under the table as all those

aforementioned soft spots started to melt. "That was not a blindfold. That was my T-shirt."

"More coffee, sir?" The prim waitress's gaze darted back and forth between the two of them as if waiting for one of them to sprout horns—probably Beau.

"Yes, please, ma'am."

His wicked grin had spread over his face, and the waitress blushed to the roots of her severely restrained hair.

When she spun around, rather too quickly, Deb kicked him again. "You're a bad boy."

"I do have those fuzzy cuffs if you want to use them."

"I think we need to get our minds out of the gutter and into Dr. Herndon's bedroom—uh, house."

Pushing back from the table, he winked and dropped several bills on the table.

Deb tapped the money. "That's an awfully big tip."

"She earned it. Her ears are going to be burning for hours."

Back in the hotel room, Beau brought up the plans for Dr. Herndon's house, and they hunched over the table together reviewing the layout. They drew green lines to several possible entrances to the house and red lines for quick escape routes.

"If anyone is staking out the house, let me take care of him…or her."

Deb's red pencil went off the table. "We're not going to leave any dead bodies behind this time, are we?"

"Not unless it's self-defense. Someone shoots at me, I'm going to shoot back. It's second nature."

"Great." She rubbed out the pencil line with the tip of her finger. "What if there's someone on the property? He's not threatening you, but he's blocking our access to Herndon's house?"

"I have a dart gun in my arsenal. Sometimes it's deadly and sometimes it's not. That will be a *not* situation."

Deb took a few steadying breaths. "If we get the plans, do I tell Zendaris? Lie? How far do we take this?"

"Far enough to get Bobby back—without compromising national security."

"You make it sound so easy, Loki."

"Anything worth having is hard, Deb. Didn't you just say something like that last night? Worth the risk? If this isn't worth the risk, I don't know what is."

She nodded. Beau always knew the right words to say. Didn't he ever stumble and fall? Didn't he ever have regrets? Didn't he ever have fears? Could she trust a man like that?

Of course, he just might regret their one-night stand when she got around to telling him about Bobby. It would break her heart if he did, but she'd have to face it. And then she'd move on.

She'd decided that giving Bobby a father had to become a priority. No more declining blind dates or brushing off the flirtations of various men at the gym, the grocery store, friends' parties.

No more daydreams about Loki—or night dreams.

She'd reveled in every second and sensation of their lovemaking last night, knowing they might not come together again. She'd have to stop comparing every man she met to Beau. It wasn't fair to the men, her or Bobby.

He needed a father, not some illusion. Not some spy on a pedestal. If Beau wanted nothing more to do with her or Bobby at the end of this game, she'd stuff her feelings down and form a relationship with someone who could be there for her and her son. Someone who could be there when the guns stopped blazing and the cars stopped screeching.

She could do it. Anything worth having was hard.

Dropping her pencil, she yawned. "I think I'm going to take a nap before lunch and finalizing these plans."

"Oh, no, you're not."

She snapped her mouth shut. "Excuse me?"

"We have a mission tonight. Your strength and agility just might save your life—and mine." He threw one of his T-shirts at her. "We're going to the gym to work out."

"You're worse than one of my Team Three members. Can we nap after the workout?"

"We can definitely go to bed after the workout."

She threw a sharp glance his way, but he'd bent over to tie his shoes.

He stood up, dragging her coat from the back of the chair and folding it over his arm. "Do you want to hang this up? Might as well straighten up a little before we leave the room to the maid."

"Sure."

He extended his arm and stopped. "Did you leave the phone in here?"

Her heart skipped a beat as she swiveled toward the desk by the computer. "I thought I left it there."

Her pulse returned to its normal rhythm when she spied her lifeline to Bobby on the other side of the laptop. "It's here. I'll take it to the gym."

Beau plunged his hand into her coat pocket and pulled out her personal cell phone. "This is your own phone, right?"

"Yeah, that's mine. Is it dead? I haven't looked

at it in days. I turned it off when I got here just in case someone wanted to use it to track me down."

He pressed a button. "Completely dead. It'll work with my charger. Do you want me to plug it in? You don't have to use it if you're afraid Prospero will ping you."

She shrugged. "Might as well. I'm not sure I want to see or hear any messages on there if they're all from Prospero."

He attached her phone to his charger and then crooked his finger at her. "No stalling. Let's go."

True to his word, Beau put her through a rigorous workout—strength, agility, balance. Not that a few hours hitting the gym would prepare her for the assignment tonight, but it bolstered her confidence.

Beau was good about bolstering her confidence. And how was she repaying him?

He came up behind her and kneaded her shoulders. "How'd that feel?"

"This feels great." She rolled her head back.

"I meant the workout."

"That felt great, too." Tipping her chin at the water dispenser, she asked, "Do you want more water?"

"Sure."

She pulled two plastic cups from the dispenser and waited for the woman in front of her to fill her water bottle.

When the woman turned, she smiled at Deb. "You and your husband have a great connection."

"My…? Yeah, we do."

"It must be nice to share interests with each other." She made a face and took a swig of water. "My husband and I don't do anything together anymore. I try to get him to be more active, but he'd rather sit in the room and read scientific journals."

Deb stepped around her to fill the cups. "Even if you liked reading scientific journals, it's not something you can do together, huh?"

"Exactly. I'm even a nurse and I don't like it. Of course, I made my husband take me to that charity ball the other night and look how that ended up."

Deb's hand jerked and the water sloshed over the edge of the cup. "Charity ball?"

The woman's eyes bugged out. "You didn't hear about that? My husband was in town for that scientific symposium on defense. That's how he got an invitation to the charity event at the end of the conference, but that big-shot scientist croaked on the dance floor."

"Oh, I did hear something about that on the news." Deb placed the cup on top of the water dispenser. "Did they ever found out the cause of death?"

"Not that I know of."

"Did your husband know Dr. Herndon?"

"Dr. Herndon?"

"The man who died."

The woman smacked her forehead with the heel of her hand. "I'd forgotten his name already. See, you know more about it than I do. No, my husband didn't know him. Of course, now my husband is using that doctor's death as an excuse to avoid parties—as if that happens every week."

"Well, I hope the rest of your visit is uneventful."

"Now, what fun would that be?" She laughed and returned to her machine.

At least the woman hadn't recognized her from the charity ball or the newspaper photo the next morning.

She handed Beau the water and he tossed it off in one gulp. "Making friends?"

Deb pitched her voice low. "Turns out she was at the little shindig the other night."

"She didn't recognize you?" He crushed the cup in his hand.

"She did not." She wiggled her fingers. "Now stop wasting cups. I'll get you a refill in that one."

"You don't have to fetch water for me, Deb."

"You gave up a lot to help me. It's the least I can do."

Later they returned to the room and scurried for the bathroom door in a mad dash. They collided and Beau wrapped his arms around her from behind, lifting her feet off the carpeted floor. He swung her around and dumped her on the bed, landing on top of her.

She panted. "Are you really going to claim the shower first after I brought you all that water?"

"Is that why you did it, so you could call dibs on the shower?"

"Actually, you go first. I want to chill out and watch TV. Maybe I'll take that nap now."

"Are you sure?" He brushed a lock of hair from her eyes. "I was just teasing about the rush to the bathroom."

She pushed at his chest. "Go, but don't be surprised if I'm sound asleep when you get out."

He kissed her nose and rolled off of her.

When the bathroom door closed behind Beau, Deb snuck a soda from the minibar and swept her newly charged phone from the table on her way back to the bed. She stretched out, hit the remote for the TV and turned on her phone. It couldn't be tracked if she just checked her messages, could it?

She scrolled through several messages from Cade, J.D. and Gage, her Prospero teammates. They'd all ganged up on her, but it didn't sound as if one of them believed she'd turned.

She kissed the display of her phone. "I love you guys."

She also had several voice mails, and the ones from Jack Coburn didn't sound all that warm and fuzzy.

When the next voice mail started, the voice of Bobby's pediatrician surprised her. "Deb, this is Dr. Nichols. Give me a call as soon as you can. We got those test results back for Bobby."

A little fizz of fear touched the back of her neck. The test results? Dr. Nichols hadn't made a big deal about them at the time of the visit—just some blood, some urine. No big deal.

In the next voice mail, Dr. Nichols's voice sounded more urgent. "Deb, this is Dr. Nichols again. I need to speak to you about Bobby's test results. I don't want to worry you too much, but it is imperative we talk."

Well, Doc, you just worried me.

Deb held her breath and pressed two to hear the next message.

"Deb, I hope everything is all right. It's not like you to ignore any issues with Bobby's health, and well, this is an issue. We need to speak."

With dread pounding against her temples, she punched the button for the next message.

"Dr. Nichols here. Typically, I wouldn't go into this on the phone, but you need to hear this information about Bobby's test results. His blood tests indicated an immune deficiency. That's why he's getting sick so much. This is definitely not as serious as it could be, but Bobby's going to need some blood, and we both know that's not going to be easy with his O negative type."

The doctor explained a few more details that would've made much more sense in person where she could've asked some questions. But she couldn't be there. She was in Boston. And Bobby was with strangers. Sick. In need of blood. Blood she couldn't give him.

The bathroom door opened. "I thought you'd be sleeping by now."

Beau padded into the room on bare feet and halted. "Deb, is everything okay?"

She had the phone clasped between her knees and she raised her eyes to meet Beau's worried gaze. "No. Everything just went from bad to worse."

His gaze darted from the phone she'd left on the bed to the one in her hands. "Not Zendaris?"

"Bobby's pediatrician has been trying to reach me."

"Why?"

"Bobby's sick."

"Oh, Deb." He crossed the room and crouched beside her. "Is it serious? Is that why he's been feeling under the weather?"

"I don't know how serious it is, but he mentioned an immune deficiency. I need to talk to the doctor."

"But not HIV or something like that?" He placed a hand on her bouncing knee.

"N-no. He mentioned that this illness is not as serious as it could be, so it sounds like it can be treated."

"That's encouraging. Now we just need to get him home and get that treatment for him."

"You don't understand." She knotted her fingers and the phone dropped to the floor and bounced once.

"I know it seems like a long shot to get him back without giving Zendaris the plans, but we can do it."

"It's not that, Beau. It's the treatment."

"What is it? Some type of blood or platelet transfusion? It's not gonna be pleasant, but I'm sure he'll pull through."

"Something like that, but Bobby has an uncommon blood type, O negative, and he needs to get blood from another O negative donor."

A deep furrow formed between Beau's eyebrows. "That's a crazy coincidence. I have the same blood type."

"I know that. I figured you did."

He sat back on his heels, his hand sliding from her knee.

"I figured you did because you're Bobby's father."

Chapter Thirteen

The room spun around him. Hell, the world tilted.

He was a father? He was Bobby's father? He didn't doubt Deb. The timing worked out, although Bobby had to be older than she'd claimed. He hadn't just turned two; he must be almost two and a half. The picture of his nephew, Zach, his older brother's kid, looked just like Bobby in Deb's picture. How had he missed that?

This also meant Deb hadn't run back to her lover or boyfriend, probably hadn't had a boyfriend at all.

It also meant she'd lied. For over two years she'd kept his son from him and then she'd kept the truth from him for over two days now.

And now his son was sick and being held captive.

"Say something."

His gaze returned to her face, strained with worry, her eyes bright with unshed tears. He swallowed the angry words that rose to his lips. "Why didn't you tell me?"

She flinched.

He'd suppressed the angry words, but his fury must've seeped into his tone.

Spreading her hands in her lap, she said, "There were a few reasons, Beau. First, I didn't even know Beau Slater was your name. You were always Loki to me. You were Loki that night."

"Cop-out."

She flinched again.

"You're an intelligence expert. There was any number of ways you could've discovered the identity of Loki. Next?"

Her fingers twisted, but she held his gaze. "Okay, you're right. Maybe I could've figured out your real name. Then what? Presented a pregnancy to a man who'd made it clear he didn't want to be tied down? A man who reveled in the spy's life—a different country every week, no home, no family obligations, freedom?"

Her words pricked him—right between the eyes. He must've really gone overboard with the James Bond stuff that night.

"Good God, Deb. That was one-night-stand pillow talk. Did you really believe I was that shallow?"

"That's my third point." She held up three fingers as if to prove it. "I was embarrassed. We had a glorious, passionate encounter for one night. And then I was supposed to present you with a son nine months later? I wasn't some giddy girl who didn't understand the ins and outs of conception. I should've used protection."

"If it comes to that, *I* should've been using protection. That's not the point. You didn't, I didn't and we produced a baby. And then you kept him from me for over two years."

She jumped up from the chair and took a turn around the room. "I didn't know how you'd take the news."

"Doesn't matter. It's not up to you to control my feelings. Stop trying to control everything." He grabbed the pillow from the chair and threw it across the room.

She ducked, even though he'd tossed the pillow in the opposite direction.

"I was scared, Beau. I was afraid that I'd present you with our beautiful boy and you'd reject him. I couldn't bear that for my son. Not my son." She swiped the back of her hand across her cheek.

Was she bringing up her own abandonment to soften him up? The hard knot that had formed in the pit of his stomach when she'd told him about Bobby loosened.

Squeezing his eyes closed, he pinched the bridge of his nose. He'd risen from his crouch when he threw the pillow and now they stood across the room from each other, the air between them crackling with emotion.

"I understand about your fears. I do. But you brought a child into this world alone. What did you put on his birth certificate for his father? Unknown? Isn't that *your* father's name?"

Her face crumpled and a sob ripped through her body, making her slump forward. "It was hard, but I thought it would be even worse if you knew about him and rejected him. I—I thought I could find a father for him one day."

Anger pounded against his temples and he smacked his chest with his fist. "I'm his father."

"I'm sorry." She raised one arm, her fingers stretched out toward him. "I should've tracked you down. I should've told you from the beginning. I see that now. I see how you talk about your nieces and nephews, but you didn't reveal that side of yourself to me in our first meeting."

He tensed his muscles, steeling himself against her gesture. Instead of going to her, which every fiber of his being wanted to do, he snorted. "Our first meeting was a hot tangle of body parts. My nieces and nephews didn't come up."

She dropped her arm and hugged herself. "I told you about my life—the foster homes, the trouble, Robert."

"Last time I checked, you're a woman. Chicks talk."

She rolled her eyes and the hug turned into arms crossed over her chest. "Oh, you talked,

Loki. You talked about the fight you had on the streets of Istanbul. The cat-and-mouse game you played with the Russian spy in the halls of the Kremlin. The Saudi princess who stripped for you in her father's palace. You talked about the high life. The spy's life. You didn't sound like father material."

His skin prickled with heat. He wanted to ram his fist into the wall. He cleared his throat. "Pillow talk."

"It left an impression."

He wouldn't let her turn this around on him. She'd made the choice, and although he could understand that choice better, it didn't change the facts.

"You should've told me, Deb."

"I know. I see that now. I saw it when you talked about your family. I made a big mistake." She swept her hands across her face. "Will you help Bobby?"

"If you have to ask that, you don't see a thing."

DEB LET THE water from the shower trickle down her face to join the tears and wash them away.

She'd screwed up. Big-time.

All the reasons she'd given herself for not tracking down Bobby's father turned to ash when confronted with Bobby's father.

She'd allowed her fantasies of Loki to sway

her. The stories he'd told her in bed hadn't done anything to disavow her of those fantasies. He was everything she'd imagined him to be.

Just not father material.

She hadn't been looking for a father for her children that night. She'd been looking for a good time. She'd been looking for a hookup with a man she'd dreamed about for two years, ever since she'd read about one of his exploits in a journal.

She hadn't been mother material that night, either. Beau was right—chicks talk. And she'd talked about a dysfunctional childhood being shuttled from foster home to foster home. Anti-social behavior. Thieving and lying. And finally being taken in hand by a tough ex-marine who'd lost his own daughter to a drug overdose.

If she were a man looking for a mother for his children, she would've run the other way after meeting her.

Sighing, she cranked off the water. They still had to get through this assignment together. She knew he had her back…and Bobby's. The fact that she'd even questioned his commitment put the nail in the coffin of any kind of relationship they might have had.

But he'd be there for Bobby.

She knew that now. Beau Slater would never abandon his son, no matter what his son's mother had done or how she'd insulted him.

They'd planned to get a bite to eat before setting off for Herndon's house. She'd gladly eat crow just to sit down with Beau and try to explain herself again. Not that it would do any good at this point.

She toweled off and dressed in the bathroom. Then she poked her head out the door. She didn't know what she expected to find—Beau sitting in a corner gnashing his teeth or standing on the balcony throwing pillows into the river.

He waved her over from where he was hunched over the laptop. "Found something interesting on our bookstore guy."

The tightness in her chest eased and she strolled to the corner of the room and looked over his shoulder. The screen showed a page from the beefy man's passport.

"Quite the world traveler, isn't he?" Her voice sounded high and unnatural so she cleared her throat.

"Look at this." Beau jabbed at the display. "Didn't one of your guys track Zendaris down to a house in Colombia recently?"

"Gage Booker. He raided his compound down there, although Zendaris had already fled. That's where he found the nanny."

"This guy, Damon, was in Colombia recently. We can say with a fair amount of certainty that this man is in Zendaris's employ, and he's the one who left the invitation for you."

"It helps getting an ID and confirmation that he's Zendaris's man. Now if we could just see him again, we could follow him or get a jump on him."

"Exactly."

"Good job, Beau." She touched him awkwardly on the shoulder and then snatched her hand back. "I think I'll watch TV for a bit and then, um, did you want to get something to eat?"

Squinting, he brought his face close to the laptop where he'd brought up another document. "I think it's best if we eat in the room. We may have identified Damon here, but we still don't know the driver of the SUV yesterday."

"You're right." She backed up to the bed and sat up against the pillows against the headboard while she clicked on the TV. "Is the TV too loud?"

"No."

The hotel maid had done a good job of swapping out the sheets and making the bed, erasing all evidence of the passionate sex she and Beau had shared here less than twenty-four hours ago. Her clumsy declaration to Beau that he was Bobby's father had done a good job of erasing the rest.

She scanned through the channels, skipping

over the local evening news. She didn't need to add to her depression anymore.

She stopped the channel at a cartoon with a silly sponge and a dumb-as-rocks starfish—one of Bobby's favorites. She giggled at their antics.

Several minutes later, Beau tilted his chair back to get a view of the TV. "What are you watching?"

"A cartoon—the sponge guy is trying to raise money with a singing contest, and his friend, the starfish, wants to enter but he's just so bad." She laughed again as Beau raised his brows. "I guess it's funnier when you know the characters."

"You know these characters?"

"Heck, yeah."

"Does Bobby watch this cartoon?"

"It's one of his favorites. That's their friend. He's an uptight squid."

Beau watched the cartoon through two commercial breaks, studying it as closely as he'd been perusing those documents on the laptop. Then he shook his head and resumed his research on the computer.

When the show ended, Deb flipped over to some comedy show rerun and dropped the remote on the bed. "Do you want me to order dinner?"

"Sure." He reached across the laptop and flipped open the room service menu. "Get me the steak, no potato, extra asparagus instead. Have them send up a pitcher of iced tea, too."

He tossed the menu at the bed and she dove for it before it hit the floor. She ran her finger down the columns of food.

Beau stretched and grabbed the handle of the balcony door. "You should get the...never mind."

He slid open the door and stepped outside. Leaning over, he folded his arms across the flat wooden barrier around the porch.

Deb picked up the phone and ordered a steak for herself, too. She wanted to match Beau stride for stride tonight. She didn't want him accusing her of holding them back. Of course, for that accusation, there'd have to be some passion involved and right now Beau was treating her like a casual stranger.

She studied him through the sliding door. The wind ruffled his short hair, and his strong profile stood out against the blue sky.

Was he thinking about their plan tonight or was he thinking about Bobby? Maybe he was thinking about both because if the mission didn't work out, he may never get the opportunity to meet his son.

Stop. She covered her mouth with her fist, biting into her knuckle. She couldn't think that way. It was counter-productive and flew in the face of everything Prospero had taught her. The mission had to succeed. There was no room for failure. There was no other outcome.

He stayed on the balcony until the food arrived. When the knock came on the door, he stepped into the room and retrieved his weapon from beneath the bed.

He used the same M.O. as he had a few nights ago. When he peeled his eye away from the peephole, he opened the door and rolled the cart into the room.

Instead of laying out their food on the table for the two of them, he took his own plate from the cart and brought it to the table where the computer sat.

She got it. He didn't want to eat with her. He could barely look at her.

She dragged the cart toward the bed, poured a glass of iced tea from the pitcher and placed it at his elbow.

"Thank you."

"You're welcome."

Then she plopped onto the bed and ate her steak from the cart. She didn't even like steak, but figured it would please Beau to eat what he was eating to prepare for the mission. Fat lot of good it did her.

She should've figured out two years ago that it would've pleased Beau if she'd told him they had a son together.

Beau shoved his half-eaten steak to the side of the table and leaned over to hoist the pitcher from the cart. "More tea?"

"No, thanks."

The brown liquid streamed into his glass, and the tinkling ice was the only sound breaking the silence between them. Facing the cops, a security system and a rottweiler at Herndon's house would be preferable to the strained atmosphere in this room.

Beau stirred some sugar into his tea and took a long drink, draining half the glass. "I have a black jacket you can wear and a black wool cap."

"Okay."

"We'll try the entrance we discussed first, and if there's a problem there we go around the back to our second option. Agreed?"

"Agreed."

"The most likely place for these plans in a house would be a safe. We'll search for a safe first. If there are any laptops in the house, we'll take them."

"Good idea."

"Once the police determine foul play in Herndon's death, they'll be all over his house. They may have already taken his computers."

"You're right."

"Deb." He plowed his fingers through his hair. "I don't need a yes-man. I need someone to bounce ideas off. I need someone to challenge and correct me."

She dropped her fork on her plate. "I just want to make it up to you, Beau."

"Ordering steak and saying yes to everything I throw out there is not going to make up for keeping my son a secret from me."

"I'm trying. I just want to explain…"

He sliced a finger across his throat. "Save it. I already told you I'm going to help Bobby, right now—tonight, and when he comes home by donating my blood or whatever else he needs. I'll be there for him. You don't need to worry about that."

Would he be there for her, too? Somehow, looking into his frosty blue eyes, she didn't think so. It had to be enough that he'd be a part of Bobby's life.

"Thanks. He's a wonderful little boy."

"And stop thanking me. It's what any father would do for his child."

"Not necessarily." She stabbed her fork into the steak.

His tone softened. "It's what this father would do."

She shoved the cart out of her way and brushed past Beau. Hovering over the laptop, she said, "What are we going to do if the neighbor on this side of Herndon's property has security lights? And are we going to search together or split up? Together is safer—apart is faster."

He joined her at the computer, careful not to touch her as if she had cooties.

She tried not to inhale his scent, tried not to notice his strong hands hovering over the keyboard.

Nodding, he said, "That's what I need from you."

And I need so much more from you.

A few hours later, they were ready to roll.

They'd packed their equipment in a backpack and stashed it in the trunk of Deb's car—the car Zendaris had provided for her getaway. The drive out to Herndon's house took just over thirty minutes.

Beau cruised past the house first. The leafy suburb provided some generous space between the houses.

Deb said, "At least the houses aren't right on top of each other. I don't think any neighbor casually looking out his window is going to see us breaking into Herndon's place."

"Or going to hear a breaking window."

"They will hear an alarm, though, so we'd better make sure that system is deactivated."

Beau parked the car around the corner. "Are you ready to make a run for it if we have to?"

"Didn't I tell you I used to run track in high school?"

"You told me you used to run from the cops in high school."

"That's why I was so good at track." She winked and coaxed one small quirk of the lips out of him. That was the first thing remotely related to a smile she'd seen since she'd told him the news about Bobby.

Beau pulled the pack out of the backseat and hung it over one arm as he exited the car. Deb followed, easing her door shut. A dog barked in the distance but not because he'd heard any slamming car doors.

The soles of their tennis shoes whispered on the bare pavement. If this had been fall instead of winter, multicolored leaves would be crunching beneath their feet. Occasionally, a brown leaf skittered across the road.

Deb had tucked her hair into the cap and had zipped Beau's jacket up to her chin. If anyone did spot her, they'd see a floating white oval in the black of night.

They reached Herndon's house and crept along the side of the front lawn. They located the low window on the side of the house that led to a back bedroom in the house.

Beau fished a glass-cutting tool and suction cup from his bag and sliced a neat square at the top of the window near the lock. He attached the suction cup to the glass and pulled, removing the glass with no muss and no fuss.

Deb whispered, "You could be a cat burglar."

He reached into the space with his long fingers and flicked the lock. "Now let's just hope he hasn't further secured the window with a bolt."

He pushed on the window sash and after a little resistance, it slid up.

As planned, Deb hoisted herself through the window, flicked on her penlight and sailed through the sparsely furnished bedroom. She turned to the left, located the mudroom and unlocked the door.

When Beau appeared out of the darkness, she jumped, banging her elbow on the washing machine.

"Careful." He steadied her by placing a hand on her back. "Let's find his office first, check for computers and safes, and then look for other likely locations for safes."

"The room I entered looked like a spare bedroom. We can skip that one."

The beam of his flashlight led the way out of the mudroom and back to the hallway. They poked their heads into the other rooms off the hallway, but Herndon had used them all as bedrooms. A smaller room off the living room contained a desk and shelves crammed with books and binders.

"Bingo." Beau swept the room with his flashlight.

A computer monitor sat on the desk, but cables dangled where it would have been attached to a CPU.

Deb pointed at the tangled cables. "Do you think the cops took that?"

"Herndon died two days ago. It's probably going to take the cops a little longer to get the approval to search his premises."

"Maybe he sent it out for repair or didn't even use it." She scanned the desk. "Is there a laptop instead?"

"Nothing. There's no computer in this office."

They rifled through the desk drawers, which Herndon hadn't bothered to lock. They checked in the small closet, but Herndon's messy office held no secrets.

Beau asked, "You okay to fan out?"

"I'll backtrack to his bedroom, and you can take the front of the house. I saw some paintings in the living room—perfect place for a wall safe."

"Whistle if you find something."

Deb sidled along the hallway, trailing one hand along the wall. She skipped the two spare bedrooms and headed straight for Herndon's private lair.

She went for the closet first and shoved aside the Oxford shirts and tweed jackets to search the floor of the closet. Shoes took up most of the space on one side and boxes of papers and awards on the other. He could've buried the plans under this meaningless stuff to throw off any potential thieves. Thick dust coated her fingers where she'd moved the boxes, so it didn't seem likely he'd hidden something here in the past several months.

She sat back on her heels, wiping the grime from her gloved fingers on the carpet. Dr. Herndon wouldn't mind now.

Her gaze skimmed the small pictures on the walls, too small to conceal a wall safe. She checked anyway.

The king-size bed dominated the room with its four posts and deep blue bedspread. It figured, since Dr. Herndon had been quite the ladies' man. He'd probably had his share of young, eager female students in this room.

A flat-screen TV faced the bed, and surround-sound speakers stared down from each corner of the room. He even had a small refrigerator tucked into a credenza with glasses lining the shelf.

Ducking down, she swung open the fridge and two bottles of wine clinked together. She stared at the books on the nightstand with headphones hooked over the drawer. He'd spent a lot of time in this room.

She dropped to her hands and knees. Robert had stored lots of stuff beneath his bed—even cash—said he trusted his bed more than a bank. Deb crawled to the bed and flipped up the bedspread. She reached for a long case and knew before she unzipped it she'd find a rifle.

A wooden box was cozied up next to the edge of the nightstand and she pulled it toward her. The small lock that secured it was child's play for her knife. She flipped up the lid and gasped.

Explicit photos of women in varying stages of bondage littered the top layer of the box. She shuffled them to the side and curled her fingers around the papers beneath.

The footfall on the carpet behind her caused prickles to run across the back of her neck. She held her breath, waiting to hear Beau's low, sexy voice.

She didn't.

Chapter Fourteen

"Get your hand away from the knife and move to the left, Agent Sinclair."

Beau drew back from the door. The man holding Deb at gunpoint obviously had no idea Deb had company in the house. Good.

The man blocked Beau's view of Deb, but he heard a rustling noise. She'd better not try anything stupid like go for her knife.

Beau took one silent, stealthy step to the right to line up behind the guy. While their unwelcome visitor was giving some other instruction to Deb, Beau was at his back in two long strides.

With one hand he gripped the back of the man's neck, squeezing with all his strength. With the other he knocked his gun hand to the ceiling.

The man didn't even get a shot off. He dropped to his knees, the gun falling from his hand.

Deb lunged for her knife and jumped to her feet. She kicked the gun away from the man's reach.

He wouldn't be needing it anyway.

Beau hoisted the backpack over his shoulder and snatched the gun from the floor. "Let's get out of here. Now."

"Is he dead? Did you break his neck?"

"With my fingers?" He snorted. "I cut off the blood flow through his carotid artery. He's out, but he'll be coming to soon, and this one usually works with a partner."

"You know him?" The whites of her wide eyes shined in the dark.

"Yes. Now move."

They crawled out through a different window in case someone was watching the mudroom door or the broken side window. When they hit the ground, they did an army crawl away from Herndon's property.

Grass, leaves and dirt clung to Beau's clothes as he crawled after Deb, silently urging her on. She'd been the complete professional all night. The atmosphere had been tense between them, but she'd never lost her focus.

He couldn't say the same for himself. Bobby weighed heavy on his mind all night—his son. What if his immune deficiency disease got the better of him before they could rescue him? What if he never got to meet him? After the failure of tonight, that possibility was too real to contemplate.

Ever since Deb broke the news to him, he'd

wanted to see his son's picture again but he was too proud to ask. Or too stupid. He wanted to know everything about him. Now the only way he might know Bobby was through secondhand accounts.

No. He couldn't let that happen.

They found themselves in the backyard of the next property. This one hugged the corner lot, and if they got through the rest of this yard they'd be close to the car.

Deb had figured out the same thing. She twisted her head around and pointed to the side.

The tangle of foliage finally ended at the edge of a manicured lawn. They continued their crawl across the dew-soaked grass and skirted the brick patio. A wooden fence separated the yard from the street and they hopped it, landing on the dirt path that passed for a sidewalk in this area.

The car was waiting for them, unmolested. Beau didn't want to alert anyone along the street, so he held off on using the remote until they got to the doors. They slid inside and he tossed the pack into the backseat. Without turning on the headlights, he started the car and shot off down the road.

They didn't speak for several minutes, their panting filling the car, steam rising from their bodies.

Beau hurtled toward the freeway, careening

along the on-ramp. A few cars whizzed past them, but nobody else had gotten on the freeway where they did.

Beau broke the silence. "That guy was my replacement."

"Where do you know him from?"

"Security circles. Coburn didn't waste any time. He may have already had the guy lined up before he even spoke to me. Who knows? He could've even traced my cell phone."

"How'd he figure we'd be at Herndon's house?"

"Coburn had already put two and two together. I told him you were in the Boston area and then Dr. Herndon winds up dead in the Boston area. The guy was probably just staking out Herndon's house."

"Jack's going to know you're helping me." She pulled the black cap from her head and the static electricity made her hair stand out at the sides.

"Yep." He squeezed her thigh because he just couldn't help himself despite his hands-off policy. "I'm sorry, Deb."

"Sorry? What for?"

"I'm sorry we got interrupted in our search. Sorry we won't be able to give Zendaris what he wants—for now. But we'll get another chance. I'll make sure of it."

"Oh, yeah, that." She reached inside her jacket

and pulled out a sheaf of papers. A few photos fell into her lap.

"Is that what I think it is?"

She waved the papers in the air. "I have the anti-drone plans."

BACK IN THE hotel room, they sat across from each other on the bed, passing the papers back and forth. Beau was no scientist or engineer, but he trusted Deb when she told him this is what she'd been briefed on to look for.

"I can't believe he had these plans underneath his bed. Maybe that's where we should hide them until we get them into secure hands."

She tapped the edge of one of the photos on a piece of paper. "How are we going to get these into secure hands and get Bobby back from Zendaris?"

"We'll wait and see how he wants to do the exchange before we come up with a plan."

"Bobby needs to get back home to start his treatment. The doctor indicated he'd be at risk for all kinds of viruses if we don't."

"I promise you, we will." He toyed with one of the pictures Deb had found with the plans. "I guess Dr. Herndon liked to keep all his dirty little secrets in one place."

"I told you he was kind of a perv." She peered at one of the photos. "But it looks like everyone is a consenting adult and thoroughly enjoying himself or herself."

"Especially her." He flicked a photo in Deb's direction.

She pinched it between two fingers, her eyes widening. "Oh, my God."

"What?" He rose to his knees and took another look at the picture. "This one is no more extreme than the others. It just looks like she's really getting into her dominatrix role."

"I know her." Deb tapped the photo.

"You're kidding. What are the chances of that?"

"No, I *know* her. She sold or gave the plans to Herndon."

"This woman in black leather and thigh-high boots is the one who stole the plans from Stark?"

"Abby Warren—turns out she was a psycho, not just a garden variety traitor."

"Uh-oh, you don't want a woman holding a whip to be a psycho."

Deb dropped the picture. "She led Zendaris on—promised to give the plans back to him when she'd probably already sold them to Herndon."

"Somehow I find it hard to muster up much sympathy for Zendaris. Someone cheated him at his own game—good for Mistress Abby. Someone's about to cheat him again."

"I hope he calls soon." She plugged the Zendaris phone into the charger and rolled up the plans. "We can't stash these under a hotel bed. Where should we hide them?"

"Can't we just burn them?" He snapped a rubber band around the tube.

"I have to turn them over to Prospero. It would be a feather in Jack's cap to produce these plans for the Department of Defense. Weapons experts can study them to find out how to fortify the drone missile against deactivation."

"You care that much about Prospero and Jack? He just sent a guy to capture you."

"He's just doing his job." She uncrossed her legs and dangled them off the side of the bed. "He sent you to me, too, and for that I'll forever be grateful to him."

"I think you would've figured a lot of this out on your own, Deb. In the end, you're the one who found the plans under Herndon's bed."

She folded her hands in her lap and kicked her legs. "I wasn't referring to the assignment. He sent you to me and you couldn't have been a more perfect person at a more perfect time. You offered to help me and help Bobby without even knowing he was yours."

"I could see how torn up you were about his kidnapping. A man would have to have a heart of stone to turn away from you." He traced the straight line of her spine.

"It was fate that Jack hired you before he hired that man back at Herndon's house. If he'd been the one tracking me from the jewelry store heist, Bobby would be dead. Bobby got his father when he needed his father most."

"I'd like to think that amateur would've never pinpointed your location like I did."

"He's not going to call tonight. It's almost midnight."

Deb scrambled to her feet and jumped up and down on top of the bed, scattering the kinky pictures. "I don't know about you, but I'm wound up so tightly I can't sleep."

Adrenaline pumped through Beau's system, fast and hot and unwanted. Was this Deb's invitation to a repeat performance of last night? As much as he'd enjoyed that performance, they needed to settle a few things first.

He grabbed her ankle. "You've got surplus energy? How about telling me about my son? Show me that picture again and any others you might have on your phone. Let me in on the phone call tomorrow morning with his pediatrician, so I can learn about this illness, too, and what I need to do to make it better for him."

Her cheeks flushed a pretty pink, whether from her trampoline jumping or his request, he couldn't tell. She bounced to her knees and grabbed her purse off the floor.

"Do I have pictures."

She started at the beginning with the same picture she'd shown him in her wallet with her holding a newborn Bobby in the hospital.

She talked his ear off the rest of the night and into the morning, regaling him with stories of Bobby's first smile, first step, first word—all the things he'd missed.

He soaked it all in now, feeling as proud of all of Bobby's accomplishments as if he were… his father.

Deb's manic pace slowed. She'd shown him every picture she had of Bobby. The stories got sillier and sillier as her lashes drooped over her green eyes.

When the phone slipped from her hand and her head slumped to one side, Beau tugged the covers down and helped her crawl underneath. He joined her, fully clothed as she was.

He slipped an arm around her shoulders and pulled her close until her head bobbed to his chest. As he stared into the face of this mom who'd gone to hell and back for her son and had managed to recover the plans to the anti-drone, he realized he was looking at Superwoman.

And even Superwoman made mistakes sometimes.

The next morning, Deb had already slipped out of bed and showered by the time he opened even one eye. He watched her stuffing her dirty clothes into a hotel laundry bag.

"Are you still running on adrenaline?"

She dropped the bag. "You were sound asleep a minute ago. It was the first time I'd been awake before you, so I thought I'd take advantage of it."

"If you're sending stuff to the hotel laundry, I'd like to include the clothes I wore last night." He yanked up the bedsheets and peered underneath. "The maid is going to wonder what the heck we were doing in here with all this dirt."

She kicked something on the floor. "We'd better pick up these, too, or we'll really have her wondering."

He leaned over the bed to find Herndon's private pics littering the floor. "You'd better save the one of Abby Warren. It shows how Herndon possibly got his hands on the plans."

"What do you think he was going to do with them?" She dropped to her hands and knees and started gathering the photos.

"I don't think his intentions were good or he would've immediately turned them over to the U.S. government. Maybe he was trying to sell them back to Zendaris and that's how Zendaris knew he had them."

She straightened the stack of pictures by rapping their edges on the nightstand. "If that was his plan, he was naive. You don't double-cross a man like Nico Zendaris."

"A man who takes photos like this—" he tapped the top picture of a woman with her hands secured behind her back and a gag in her mouth "—is not naive."

She flicked her fingers in the air. "That's sex. He was dabbling in high-stakes espionage, and he was in way too deep."

"He paid the price." He lifted the receiver from the hotel phone. "Are you going to call Dr. Nichols now?"

"Don't you want to take a shower first?" She wrinkled her nose. "Besides, I don't think we're going to get to talk to Dr. Nichols on the first call, especially on a Monday morning. We'll leave a message, he'll call back. That's the way it usually works."

He threw back the covers and rolled from the bed. "Okay, put the call in, but don't start without me. If he calls back while I'm in the shower, drag me out."

"You got it." She placed the call and as she'd predicted, the nurse told her the doctor would call her back as soon as he was finished with his current patient.

Beau rushed through his shower, and while he was running his hands through his wet hair in front of the mirror, the hotel phone rang.

He stumbled out of the bathroom, and Deb waited until he'd joined her at the table before picking up the phone on the third ring.

"Hello?"

"Deb? It's Dr. Nichols."

Since the hotel phone didn't have a speaker option, Beau had tilted his head against Deb's to hear the conversation.

"I didn't get back to you sooner because I've been out of the country."

"How's Bobby doing?"

"He has some flu-like symptoms."

"That's to be expected. His defenses are down and he's susceptible to everything right now."

"Can you explain his problem again to me now that I have you on the phone and can ask some questions?"

"Of course."

"Bobby's father is listening in."

Dr. Nichols paused. "I thought he was out of the picture."

"He's back in it now, and he's going to be Bobby's donor since he's also O negative."

"That's good news. I like seeing families come together like this."

The doctor explained about the immune system in layman's terms, and described Bobby's condition, treatment and prognosis.

Beau held Deb's hand through it all. It sounded

scary but the doctor assured them Bobby's disease was treatable and eventually curable.

"So, when can you come in for a consultation? I want to outline everything for you, there are some forms to sign and we want to test your blood, Mr., ahhh, Mr...."

"Slater."

"Mr. Slater. We want to make sure you're compatible with Bobby and get all the paperwork done. So call for an appointment within the next week, Deb."

"We will." She held up her crossed fingers.

When Dr. Nichols ended the call, Deb slumped in her chair. "We have to get him in there."

"We have the plans, thanks to you. We should have this wrapped up within a week."

"I'm just anxious to know how that's going to happen. I assume Zendaris is going to designate some meeting place, maybe even where they've been holding Bobby all this time."

Leaning forward, he gripped both of her knees. "You're not going into any kind of dangerous situation."

She rolled her eyes at him. "It's too late for that, Beau. This whole thing reeks of danger."

"I think you should insist on a public place."

"You know he'll never go for that. He's not going to shoot me...or anyone else in public if things don't work out his way. He'd be stuck if we were in a public place."

"You won't be going in alone anyway. I'll be right behind you, one way or the other."

"We won't be able to trick him with the plans. He's seen them before, and he won't release Bobby until he gets a look at them. If we give him something fake, he'll realize it right away."

Beau rubbed his jaw. "It would be nice if the plans were a couple of lines or a formula. Then we could rewrite it in disappearing ink or paper that disintegrates."

"That would be a great joke, but you're right, it would take forever to copy those plans."

"So, we hand them off and somehow get them back."

"Do you really think he's going to let them out of his sight again after all he's been through? He thought he had them once when he had one of his minions track down Abby Warren's former roommate. Turns out Abby tricked him, and us, and had already done her modeling at that point for Dr. Herndon and had turned them over to him. Zendaris is not going down without a fight this time."

"I guess we just have to wait until he contacts you before we can figure out how to handle this."

"I wish he'd hurry up. You'd think he'd be antsy to find out how the operation went last night."

Beau gestured to his phone next to the computer. "Coburn knows how it went."

"What do you mean?" Deb grabbed his phone and examined it. "Shouldn't this thing be turned off? He'll ping it and track you down."

"Not this phone—untraceable." He held out his hand and she dropped the phone in his palm. He punched a button and held out the phone for her to read Jack's text message.

She read it aloud. "'You're helping Deb? You turned?' Followed by two question marks."

"Which means he doesn't really believe it."

"Two question marks told you that?"

"Coburn's not a man given to excess emotion. Two question marks mean a lot."

"He doesn't believe you turned, but he knows you were with me at Herndon's house last night? His agent must've reported in with the bad news."

"Deb, I don't think he believes you turned."

"He sent not one, but two hired guns after me. Even if the second one was pretty useless, that's still a big commitment on Jack's part."

"He wants to bring you in. At no time did he ever give me any license to harm you."

"It doesn't make a difference. I can't allow him to bring me in."

"We have the plans."

"We don't have Bobby."

Her mouth formed into a stubborn line and he

knew she wouldn't listen to his scheme right now. Maybe she'd never be ready to hear it. Maybe he had to set it into motion without her knowledge.

Hell, it's not like she hadn't been deceiving him for almost three years.

Deb rose from her chair and stretched. "I am so sick of being cooped up in this hotel room. I'd really like some fresh air."

"I don't know if that's such a great idea. For a minute there last night, I thought we'd come face-to-face with your shadow, the man who's been taking potshots at you."

"Maybe he beat us to the punch. Maybe he's the one who stole Herndon's desktop computer. He searched the house but got focused on the computer and never looked in the right places."

"How did you come to look under the bed?"

"Robert used to hide things under the bed, too. He was paranoid that way." She walked to the window and peeked through the drapes.

"Despite his paranoia, he sure did a good job with you."

"He was the only father I ever knew, and he helped me so much with Bobby. He was his father figure and role model." She held up one hand. "And I'm sorry that wasn't you, Beau. It should've been you."

The realization that he'd missed those years

with his son punched him in the gut all over again. He'd have to find a way to forgive Deb and make it stick. He'd have to hold the memory of last night, when they'd talked until dawn about Bobby, close to his heart. In that moment he'd forgiven her.

He blew out a long breath. "If it wasn't me, then I'm glad it was that grizzled old marine who was there for Bobby."

"Robert told me I was wrong." She threaded her fingers together in front of her. "He told me a man deserved to know he'd fathered a child. Deserved the chance to step up. He'd gotten his wife pregnant before they married, and the day she told him she was pregnant was the day he became a man, according to him."

"You didn't listen to him?" The more he heard about Deb's surrogate father, the more he respected him.

"I didn't always take his good advice."

The hotel fire alarm blared in the room, and they both jumped at the same instant.

"What the hell?"

Deb pointed to the brightly flashing lights above the door. "This is for real."

Beau strode toward the safe in the closet. "Get the plans. I don't like this."

"It's a fire alarm."

"How many times has a fire alarm gone off in a hotel where you're staying?" He punched in the combination of the safe. "Once, twice in all the times you've stayed in a hotel?"

"You think this is a setup?"

At least she wasn't arguing with him. She grabbed the dark jacket she'd worn last night and slipped the rolled-up plans with the photo of Abby Warren inside the breast pocket.

Some shouts resounded in the hallway, and Beau peered out the peephole. "Everyone's leaving."

"We have to leave. What if it's a real fire? And even if it isn't, I'm sure security or the fire department is going to do a check of the rooms."

Who else was going to do a check of the rooms, or more specifically, this room? "It sure is an easy way to clear out all the rooms, isn't it?"

She patted her chest. "I have the plans with me. All anyone's going to find in here is a bunch of disguises and some stolen jewels in the safe. He's welcome to them. Of course, if the cops find those we'll be in a world of trouble."

"It's not the cops I'm worried about."

They joined several people in the hallway, chattering as they made their way to the stairwells.

Before one of the men swung open the stairwell door, Beau stepped in front of him. "Hold on. You should always check to see if the door's hot first."

He pressed his hand against the fire door and stepped back. "It's fine."

The man mumbled as he brushed past Beau on his way into the stairwell, "Who's he, Fireman Bill?"

Beau met Deb's dancing eyes above the hand covering her grin. "I'm sorry, but you are kind of bossy."

"Someone's gotta take charge around here."

People thronged the stairwells, the guests on the top floors pushing and shoving to get to the bottom. Beau positioned himself behind Deb to protect her from the human onslaught.

He bent forward and whispered in her ear, "I'm glad this isn't a real emergency."

Hotel personnel ushered them out a side door into the chilly morning. Guests in coats hastily thrown over bathrobes or pajamas blinked in the bright light. Others warmed their hands on coffee cups from late-morning breakfasts. Businesspeople in their suits and smart coats checked in with hotel staff and then slipped into taxis to do their morning work. A group of school kids shoved and giggled while their chaperones gave them the evil eye.

Beau tensed his muscles and scanned the crowd. Had someone pulled the fire alarm to lure him and Deb out of the hotel? The man Coburn had hired as his replacement didn't know their location if he had to stake out Herndon's house to surprise Deb.

What about Zendaris? Maybe he figured Deb had the plans and would get a jump on her before working out a trade for Bobby. His gut rolled. He did not have a lot of confidence that Zendaris would return Bobby once he got his hands on the plans.

Zendaris didn't want just the anti-drone plans. He wanted revenge on Prospero Team Three, and now he had the perfect opportunity to get it.

Someone shrieked and Beau reached for his weapon. He cranked his head around to see one of the schoolgirls in the shrubbery.

Deb patted his arm. "Easy, cowboy."

"I don't like it."

"Neither do I. It's freezing out here." She hunched her shoulders, turning up the collar of the jacket she'd borrowed from him.

Beau curled his arm around her waist and felt for the plans secured in her inside pocket. "Just don't drop these."

"And I thought you were just trying to warm me up."

"I can do that, too." He wrapped both arms

around her and pulled her close, the plans crinkling between them. She remained stiff in his embrace, probably not sure what it meant.

Hell, *he* didn't know what it meant. His feelings for her ping-ponged between anger, understanding, admiration and pure unadulterated lust.

And something else—something much more.

With the fire trucks still parked out front, hotel security waved their arms and shouted an all-clear. The hotel guests began shuffling back into the building, heading for the elevators.

Beau steered Deb back the way they'd come. "Let's take the stairs. It beats waiting in line for the elevator."

They jogged up the three flights of steps and pushed through the fire door on their floor. They'd beaten most of the other guests back inside.

Beau slid the key card into the lock and pushed open the door. He stepped back to allow Deb in first.

When the door slammed, a gust of cold air greeted them. A rash of goose pimples raced up Beau's back, but it didn't have anything to do with the temperature.

"Deb, get down." He reached for his weapon for the second time this morning, but this time it was no schoolgirl he confronted. And it was too late.

A man dressed like a firefighter emerged from

the curtained balcony, holding a gun in front of him with two hands. "We finally meet face-to-face. Now hand over those plans."

Chapter Fifteen

Deb felt the papers warm against her chest and held her breath. She could sense the tension vibrating from Beau's body.

The man pointing the weapon looked familiar, even in his firefighter disguise. *Damon.*

Zendaris was double-crossing her. He'd had no intention of returning Bobby to her. Her rage crashed through her body in hot waves, and she clenched her fists, her nails biting into her flesh.

"Slide your weapon across the floor, Loki." Damon aimed his gun at Deb's head. "Or the broad gets it right now."

Deb's pulse jumped. Zendaris had known all along that Beau had been helping her? Was that the reason for the betrayal? Had the man she'd believed was Bobby's savior turned into his destroyer?

Beau slid his weapon from his shoulder holster, placed it on the carpet and slid it across the floor. "Did Zendaris ever plan to return the boy?"

"Zendaris?" The man practically spat the word. "You still don't get it, do you?"

"What don't we get, Damon?"

The man smiled—his white teeth standing out in his brown face. "You're good, Loki. I'd heard you were the best. But I'm better."

Deb licked her lips. "Zendaris is not getting the plans until I get my son."

Damon cursed and this time he did spit. "I'm not working for Zendaris. I'm on my own now. I'm starting my own business, and it's going to start with those anti-drone plans."

Deb didn't know whether to laugh or cry. If this man got the plans from her, she'd never see Bobby again. But this was not a Zendaris double cross.

She shot a glance at Beau's stony face.

He spoke, barely moving his lips. "You work for Zendaris."

"I *did* work for Zendaris. I told you, I'm striking out on my own, and I want those plans." He wiped his mouth with the back of his hand, but his aim stayed steady. "Zendaris is supposed to be so brilliant, but I'm the one who watched this Prospero agent. I'm the one who discovered she'd hooked up with Loki. I'm the one who attached a GPS to the car Zendaris left for her."

"Does Zendaris know that?" Beau was flexing his fingers.

"Why should I tell him? *El jefe.* He wants all his peons to call him *el jefe. El pendejo* is more like it."

Beau asked, "If we have them, what do we get in exchange for the plans? Zendaris has the boy."

Damon hoisted the gun higher. "You get her life."

"Why don't you just kill me now?" Deb spread her arms wide. She'd die without Bobby anyway. "That was you who tried to shoot me at the other hotel and run me down with the car, wasn't it?"

He nodded. "I wanted you dead. I told Zendaris I could recover the plans from Dr. Herndon, but I guess he didn't trust me. I figured with you out of the way, he'd go with plan B—me. But now that you have the plans, I'll just take them from you."

He'd obviously already searched the room and hadn't found them. Deb opened her mouth to deny she had them, but Beau held up his hand.

"You killed Dr. Herndon?"

"I had to get him out of the way. I knew you two would pull some trick to make it look like Herndon died. I had to make sure it happened."

Deb threw her arms out to the side. "You were at that party, too?"

"Don't feel bad. I didn't recognize you two, either. I posed as security and then slipped some poison into those 7 and 7s he was downing faster than a sailor on leave."

"Why didn't you tell Zendaris about your accomplishment?" Beau asked.

"Why would I? He'd only wonder why I stepped in. The man doesn't trust anyone."

"If we give you the anti-drone plans now, you'll leave? You won't hurt Deb?"

"I don't care about her. Prospero's never going to get their hands on them again anyway. I already have a buyer. Give me the plans and I'll let you both go. You'll have to deal with Zendaris anyway."

"The plans aren't here."

Deb stared at the floor.

"Where are they?" Damon narrowed his eyes.

"We left them in the car."

As soon as the words were out of Beau's mouth, Deb grabbed his arm. "No. We can't give him the plans. We'll never get Bobby back."

"You're more important to me than your son. I can't lose you. I'll handle Zendaris. I'll figure out a way to get your son back."

Deb's fingertips tingled. Damn, they made a good team.

She choked out a sob.

Damon snorted. "Yeah, yeah, you'll work it out with Zendaris. Where's the car?"

"In the hotel parking lot."

"If you're lying to me, your girlfriend dies. Or maybe I'll bag Loki and start my business with some street cred."

"I'm not lying." Beau pointed to the gaping door of the safe. "You've already searched the room. You know the plans aren't here."

"Then let's get moving." Damon waved his gun. "And don't try anything on the way to the parking lot, or you're both dead and I'll find the plans myself."

They shuffled toward the stairwell with Damon behind them. Nobody saw them, but after the fire alarm nobody would look twice at a fireman walking through the hotel with two guests.

Deb hoped Beau had a good plan up his sleeve because Damon would have to pry these papers out of her cold, dead fingers.

They crossed a corner of the lobby to reach the walkway to the parking structure, receiving only cursory glances from the few people they encountered.

Damon's fireman getup clanked and squeaked as he lumbered behind them. Beau, in his dark jeans and dark jacket zipped up to his chin, looked like a long, lean panther beside Damon.

A long, lean, swift panther unencumbered and coiled to spring.

Yeah, Loki had a plan.

They climbed up one level and then two. Beau

had left the car on the second level when they'd come back from Herndon's house last night, but they continued to the third level. And beyond.

By the fourth level, Damon wiped sweat from his brow and growled. "Where is this damn car?"

"It's on the roof."

When they ascended to the top level, the wind whipped through the sparse parking lot where only a few lonely cars waited.

"Is this a joke? Your car's not up here." Damon grabbed Deb's arm and pulled her toward him, so close she could smell the coffee on his breath.

"Sure it is. It's the one on the end. Keys are in my pocket."

Damon tightened his grip on Deb. "Pull 'em out real slow or she dies right here and now."

Beau pulled a set of car keys from his pocket, dangling from his finger. They dropped to the ground.

"Oops." Before asking for Damon's approval he ducked to sweep them up.

He rose with a knife in his hand.

Deb didn't even see him swipe at Damon, but Damon grunted and his arm loosened. She plowed into his shin with her heel and ducked from his grasp.

He roared like an injured animal, and Beau slammed his arm upward with a sickening crack.

The gun dropped to the pavement, and Deb scooped it up.

By the time she rose, Damon was on his knees, his right arm hanging loosely at his side, Beau's knife against his throat.

"I guess you're not going to bag Loki." He tipped his head at Deb. "Put the gun on him, Deb."

"Done. Now where's my son, you SOB?"

"I'm not—"

Beau smacked the side of his head with his fist. "Yes, you are. Where is Zendaris keeping the boy?"

"Why should I tell you that?"

"Because if you don't, this *broad* is going to shoot you. Don't forget, she's a Prospero agent trained to kill." Beau shrugged. "And if she won't, I will."

"I'm a dead man anyway if Zendaris ever finds out about my betrayal, and he will find out if I tell you where he's stashing the kid."

"Not—" Beau ran the tip of his blade beneath one of his fingernails "—necessarily."

The big man licked his lips. "Whaddya mean?"

"If you tell us where the boy is, I can make arrangements for you, arrangements that will keep you out of Zendaris's clutches."

"How?"

"You don't need to know how. I'm Loki. Just know I can do it."

Deb's mouth watered. Damn, the man was sexy when he talked like that.

Damon's eyes shifted from the knife in Beau's hand to the gun in hers. He swallowed and nodded once. "He's holding the kid in a warehouse in Crosstown, out by the south end."

Deb clenched her teeth to hold in her scream. Zendaris had promised to keep Bobby safe. Crosstown wasn't safe. Since this whole nightmare started she'd believed only half of the stuff coming out of Zendaris's mouth—including his claim that he'd trade Bobby for the plans.

Now she had him right where she wanted him. "Address and layout."

Damon gave Beau the information, and he must've committed it to memory since he hadn't written down one word. When Damon was done, Beau turned to Deb. "Hand me the gun and take the keys to the car. Drive it up here and get my black bag out of the backseat."

She left him holding Damon at gunpoint and hoped to God nobody stumbled onto the scene. They'd have a lot of explaining to do.

She wheeled the car up to the rooftop and parked, blocking the view from the stairwell in case one of the three owners of those cars came up here.

The men were still in the same position. In fact, they looked carved from stone.

She dragged Beau's bag out of the back and unzipped it. "What do you need?"

"Rope, syringe."

Damon's legs bounced on the ground. "That doesn't sound good."

"If I wanted you dead, you'd be dead." He handed the gun to Deb again while he secured Damon's hands behind his back. "Now stand up and walk toward the car.

"Pop the trunk, Deb."

"Wait." His feet skidded to a stop. "You're not cramming me in there."

"Relax, Damon." Beau pricked the needle in the back of Damon's neck. "You won't feel a thing."

As Damon slumped forward and stumbled, Beau folded him into the trunk and covered him with blankets.

"What are we going to do with him?"

"Leave him for somebody to find."

"Not the cops. He'll be back on the streets in minutes."

"Not the cops." He slammed the trunk down on their captive.

"Not the FBI or CIA? He'll talk. Zendaris can't know about this. We have him where we want him now. We have Bobby's location, and we can get the jump on him."

He cupped her face in his hands. "It's all right, Deb. Our friend will be out for hours. By the time he comes to and I place my anonymous call, our business with Zendaris will be finished."

"How can you be so sure?"

"Look—" he smoothed his thumbs across her cheeks "—Damon's betrayal of Zendaris and his stalking of you were the best things that could've happened. To know where Zendaris has Bobby in advance of your meeting with him is priceless. We've got this."

He landed a kiss on her mouth—the first since she'd dropped the bombshell about Bobby. It felt good. It felt like a promise.

When he released her, the cold air hit her face, snapping her back to reality. They couldn't promise each other anything—not until they rescued Bobby.

She jerked her thumb at the car. "Where are we taking him?"

"I think it's safe to leave him here for now." He swept his arm across the parking lot. "Doesn't look like a lot of people park up here."

"Will he be warm enough in the trunk?"

His brows show up. "You're worried about him?"

"He gave us Bobby's location. I don't want him to die."

"He's not going to die, and if he does? He may

have given us Bobby's location at gunpoint, but he didn't seem to care what Zendaris had in store for him once you couldn't deliver the plans. I'm not going to shed any tears if the guy dies of hypothermia."

Beau moved the car to a location away from the stairwell and blasted the heat in the car just to make Deb happy. "If you want to come out here and start the engine every few hours to make sure he's warm, knock yourself out."

She clutched the phone in her pocket and dragged it out to stare at the display for the hundredth time that day. "Why hasn't he called?"

"He'll call when he's ready, which is fine because we have some work to do before he calls." He patted his chest as they descended the parking structure stairs. "You still have those plans safe and sound?"

"You were right about keeping them with us. If I'd tried to hide them in the room, Damon and the plans would be on their way to Istanbul or wherever."

He draped his arm around her shoulders. "Did I ever tell you about a fight I had in Istanbul?"

"You don't have to tell me stories." She smacked her hand against his hard stomach. "I've seen you in action, Loki. I'm a believer."

"Good. Then you're going to trust me now on

how this is going to go down." He kissed the side of her head and pulled open the door of the lobby.

She stiffened and blocked his entrance to the hotel. "I don't like the sound of that. Why are you already warning me to trust you?"

Reaching over her head, he pushed open the door. "Let's get back to the room first."

When they got to their room, Deb rounded on him. "What are you planning to do?"

"Now that we have the plans and know where Zendaris is keeping Bobby?" He aimed his fingers into a gun and shot at her. "Bring in the reinforcements."

"Reinforcements?"

He yanked his cell phone from its charger and turned it on.

"Th-they might ping you and discover our location."

"Ping away. I've already given them our location."

"What? You're bringing in Prospero?"

"Specifically, Team Three—Cade Stark, J.D. and Gage Booker."

"You already contacted them?"

"Before our fake fire alarm and they're all on their way."

She sank to the edge of the bed. "What if Zendaris finds out?"

"How's he going to find out? This is Team

Three we're talking about here. I don't know why you didn't trust them to begin with, Deb. Those guys have your back. They knew you hadn't turned." He typed a message on his phone. "I'm giving them the warehouse location now."

Fear and uncertainty swirled through her body, pumping up her adrenaline. "Unless they're lying. What if they just said that and instead they're on their way to bring me down?"

The bed dipped as he sat beside her and took her fidgeting hands in his. "Not everyone is out to bring you down. Look at Robert. You probably wondered what some old ex-marine wanted with a teenage girl he'd caught stealing from him. And all he wanted was to help you. I didn't even know Bobby was my son when I'd decided to help you. Team Three, those guys are your brothers. Let them help you, too."

"It's just—" she gripped his hands and fought the tears "—I've been doing it on my own for so long."

"You don't have to. Your brothers in arms are on the way, ready and willing to do anything to get Bobby back. And I'm here, ready and willing to be a father to Bobby—and more if you want it."

Her heart jumped, but she dared not look at his face. Did he mean he'd stick around? Want to be a family? Or had he said that to shore up her courage for the battle ahead?

She'd take it for now.

She dragged in a breath. "Where are they going to be?"

"We're not going to meet anywhere. We're doing this by secure text. I'll wait for their responses, but they'll probably move in and do surveillance on the warehouse before any meeting Zendaris sets up. We need to make sure Bobby's physically located at the property first. If they go in there with guns blazing and Bobby's not there, we'll tip Zendaris's hand."

"This is really happening." She jumped up from the bed and paced the room. "Where are they now?"

"J.D. was coming in from Colorado, Gage from Texas and Cade from Europe. Given the time zones and the fact they're all coming in on private jets, they should be here soon."

"And Jack? Does Jack Coburn know?"

"He knows."

"Why didn't you tell me?" She folded her arms and wedged a shoulder against the wall.

"I didn't want to worry you and I wasn't sure what role they could play, but as long as we had the plans I figured they had a right to know."

"I don't know whether to feel betrayed or happy."

"That's kind of how I felt when you told me about Bobby."

The pulse in her throat throbbed. "I never meant to betray you, Beau. I did it to protect myself, and yeah, because I didn't trust that you'd be there for Bobby."

He crossed the room to her slowly, his gaze never leaving her face, their electric connection as strong as it was the night their eyes first met at that bar in Zurich.

When he reached her, he curled one arm around her waist and cupped the back of her head with the other. "Woman, I know why you did it and it still pisses me off. But, God help me, it's not enough to make me give you up."

His kiss weakened her knees, and she had to cling to his neck so she wouldn't melt at his feet. His lips slid from her mouth and touched her cheeks, nose and eyes. As they hovered near her mouth again, she whispered, "I'm so sorry."

He ended her apology by sealing his lips over hers.

For the next hour, they communicated back and forth with Prospero Team Three. The three of them were on their way to Crosstown with enough ammunition and supplies to start a second revolution.

Beau assured them he'd let them know as soon as Zendaris set up the meeting. They agreed that if they got confirmation of Bobby's presence in the warehouse, they'd move in.

"I'm hoping that's the case. I really have no desire to meet Zendaris face-to-face." She toyed with the edge of the room service menu. "D-do you think even if they saw Bobby, they'd wait for the meeting so they could nail Zendaris, too?"

"I think—" he smoothed his thumb across the back of her hand "—they will do whatever it takes to secure Bobby and deal with Zendaris later. At least we have the anti-drone plans."

She shook her head to clear it of doubts. "You're right. You know, I joined the team later. One of the original members died on assignment. Jack replaced him with me. As the only woman, I always felt a little on the outside."

"Their actions today will forever prove that false." He picked up the menu. "Is it just me, or did we totally forget to eat?"

"Between fake fire drills and stuffing a fake fireman into our trunk and inviting the cavalry out to the rescue, yeah, I think we've been a little too busy to think about food."

"I'm usually never too busy to think about food." He leaned over and kissed her mouth. "Or other things."

She snatched the menu out of his hands. "When you talk like that, it makes me believe all the stories about Loki, including the ones I'd rather not think about."

"Totally exaggerated. Now let's order some room service."

"Ugh, can we go down to the restaurant to eat?"

"It's the same food. Are you getting tired of looking at my face?"

She trailed her fingers across his stubbled jaw. "Never, but now that Damon is safely in my trunk, it would be nice to get out of this room and sit at a table."

They sat across from each other in the hotel restaurant, and Beau picked up his sandwich. "Same sandwich I would've gotten upstairs."

"But we get the added bonus of listening to the couple arguing at that table and the toddler throwing his food at that one."

Beau scratched his jaw. "Does Bobby do that?"

"Occasionally."

The phone buzzed and Deb dropped her fork. *This is it.*

"It's a phone call."

"Answer it and tell him to call you back in five minutes." Beau waved for the check and stuffed two French fries in his mouth.

"Yes?"

"Do you have the plans?"

"Yes. Can you call me back in five minutes so I can have some privacy?"

He clicked his tongue. "You mean you're not holed up in your hotel room crying your eyes out?"

No, I'm working on double-crossing you.

"Five minutes."

Beau tossed some bills on the table. "Did he ask you about the plans?"

"I told him I had them."

They rushed back upstairs and just as Deb stepped inside the room, the phone rang. She answered and put it on speaker.

"What do you want me to do?"

"Meet me at the Central T stop on the Red Line. You'll be picked up and taken to your son where we'll make the exchange."

Deb laughed but it came out more like a snort through her dry mouth. "Do you think I'm stupid? You'll have me picked up and killed while you steal the plans. No, thanks. Next."

Zendaris sighed. "You really need to work on your trust issues, Agent Sinclair. If I tell you where Bobby is first, who's to say you won't enlist some help? You see, I have trust issues, too."

She rolled her eyes at Beau. "I can drive to the T stop, and you can have me followed to make sure I'm on my own. I'm not playing games. I have the plans and I want my son back."

"I think I can work with that. But we'll leave a car for you, so we can make sure there's no tracking device on it. And you'll be following another car to the location, so you're not getting the address in advance. If we pick up any tail on you, it's over."

"I'm bringing my weapon. So there'd better not be any funny business when I pick up the car or follow the other car."

"I think two distrustful people just worked out a deal. Be at the T station at nine o'clock tonight."

Zendaris ended the call, and all of Deb's strength evaporated. She sat on the floor, the phone cradled limply in her palm.

"You did it." Beau pulled her to her feet and swung her around. "The terms are great."

She finally got her mouth working. "Where will you be?"

"I'll be waiting at the warehouse. We'll all be there, waiting for you, Deb."

Covering her face with her hands, she murmured, "I'm scared. I'm scared for Bobby."

"I am, too, but this is our best chance."

She parted her fingers. "You're scared, too?"

"Damn right. I'm scared I'm never going to get the chance to meet my boy. I'm scared I'm going to lose you. I'm scared that the great Loki can't live up to his reputation."

She threw her arms around his broad shoulders. This wasn't just about her anymore. This man deserved a chance with his son, the son she'd denied him for two years.

"Don't be scared, Loki. We can do this."

Chapter Sixteen

Deb was the luckiest woman alive.

Beau surveyed the cache of weapons and explosives and equipment that Team Three had arrayed before him on the floor of the abandoned warehouse. These guys meant business.

They'd secured the abandoned warehouse on the same property as Zendaris's, coming in under the guise of a food truck making a delivery. Even if anyone at Zendaris's warehouse had seen the truck coming in, they'd put it down to commercial activity involving the food bank in the area. Plenty of food service warehouses crouched in the shadow of the Suffolk County Jail.

Not the safest place to keep a kid—unless the kid wasn't yours and you didn't give a damn about his health or safety.

He'd hated leaving Deb at the hotel to make her way to the Central T station alone, but she was no wilting flower. She had a weapon and she knew how to use it.

His place was here with her support team, and what a team it was. How could she ever have doubted these guys for a minute?

"You ever work much with explosives, Loki?" J.D. shook his head. "I mean, Slater?"

"Some. My style is more stealth."

J.D. patted the cheek of Gage Booker, the senator's son, and said, "We don't let Gage here get too close. He doesn't want to damage his pretty face."

Gage laughed. "You're the one who needs to watch out, J.D. It's your wedding coming up."

"Yeah, maybe I'd better go wait in the truck."

Cade Stark kicked up his feet on a crate while he loaded ammunition into his gun. "We haven't caught a glimpse of Deb's son yet. Make sure she realizes that when this is all over. It's not about nailing Zendaris. It's about rescuing her son."

"He's my son, too."

Silence settled over the small office space.

J.D. broke it with a whistle, and Booker coughed. "Zurich?"

"She told you?"

Booker held up his hands. "She told me she'd met you while on assignment out there, but the hotel during that time was like a spy convention. I never put two and two together when Deb announced her pregnancy."

Stark said, "Deb's on the private side. Zendaris

tried this same scheme with my son. That's why he and my wife are in Europe right now. I want nothing more than to bring this SOB down, but your boy comes first."

"I appreciate that."

Booker caressed the scope on a high-powered rifle. "You told her to get them outside, right?"

"Yeah. Zendaris knows she's skittish and even agreed to let her bring her weapon, but he'll make her give that up. She can trade her weapon for the concession of meeting outside."

J.D. checked his watch. "Gentlemen, I believe it's time we took up our positions."

Booker had the sniper's position on an opposing warehouse's rooftop. J.D. would also be on top of a warehouse with several mobile explosive devices. Stark had the peripheral area covered for any incoming personnel and to stop Zendaris's escape, if it came to that.

And Beau planned to be as close to Deb and Bobby as he could possibly be in case anything went wrong and to follow the action. He'd never admitted fear to anyone like he had to Deb this afternoon in the hotel. She had such an exalted image of the great Loki, he'd almost convinced himself that she'd turn away from him in disgust once he'd revealed how scared he was.

She hadn't.

Beau slipped out of the warehouse into the

cloudy night. A storm was brewing for tomorrow, but for tonight at least they didn't have to battle the elements. One battle was enough.

He crept along the side of the abandoned warehouse. Zendaris's people wouldn't be expecting anyone to be in the area. The deliveries had died down by five o'clock. A couple of workers from the food bank had wandered over to check on some supplies, but there had been no activity since.

Zendaris's warehouse was a hulking shape backed up to a chain-link fence. Beau dropped to his belly and crawled toward a foul-smelling Dumpster several yards from the warehouse door.

And waited.

DEB'S CLAMMY HANDS had almost slipped off the steering wheel several times during the drive, especially when she thought her guide was veering in a different direction from Crosstown. Now as she followed him through the gates of the warehouse area, she let out a pent-up breath.

Her gaze darted among the dark shapes that littered the property. Could her Team Three coworkers already be here? *Brothers,* Beau had called them—brothers in arms. If they were truly here, she'd never doubt them again.

Of course, she was leading them right to Zendaris and the anti-drone plans—something all of them thirsted for.

The car ahead of her parked in front of a windowless warehouse and she gulped. Was that where they'd been holding Bobby? She pulled in behind her escort. She left the plans on the seat of the car and scrambled from the front seat, clutching her weapon.

A pair of lights on the outside of the warehouse came on, bathing the pavement with a yellow glow. Good. They couldn't claim it was too dark to stay outside.

Stay outside. That's what Beau had told her to do.

The driver of the car didn't say a word. He stood beside the warehouse with his arms crossed. Had he taken Damon's job? Had Zendaris wondered what had happened to Damon?

He was probably being interviewed by a CIA agent about now. Beau had abandoned the car with Damon in the trunk somewhere out near Roxbury and gave the tip to Jack. In a gesture of good faith, Jack would let the CIA have a crack at Damon first.

Another car roared through the gates, cutting its lights. Deb jerked back as the car swerved next to hers.

A bald man jumped from the driver's seat and opened the back door of the black sedan. A slim man of medium height emerged, straightening the cuffs of his jacket. Deb could smell Armani.

He adjusted his dark sunglasses, tipped the brim of his fedora and smiled. "Agent Sinclair. May I call you Deb? I feel like we have such a connection."

"I feel like I have a bad taste in my mouth that I can't spit out." She raised her weapon.

He chuckled. "I have to admit, I like my women…softer, but you'd be a handful in bed. Guess you weren't that good if the father of your child abandoned you. You know a lot about abandonment, don't you, Deb? Just think, if circumstances had turned out differently and that old marine hadn't turned your life around, you could've had a job with me."

He'd picked the wrong tactics to use with her. Insults only made her stronger, fiercer. If he liked his women soft—he was gonna hate her.

"Where's my son, you slimy piece of excrement?"

"Where are my plans, you bitch?"

"I have the plans, but you're not getting them or my gun until I see my son, bitch."

He swept his arm forward. "He's inside. I'll take you to him, and you can bring the plans with you. Once I verify their veracity, I'll give you your bratty sick kid."

"No. I'm not walking into a trap." She waved

her gun. "Bring him out here, to me. I'll secure him in the car and give you the plans."

He caressed his chin as if he had a pointed beard on the end of it—like the devil. He'd sent imposters in his place before, but she was confronting the real Zendaris. She could smell it.

He snapped his fingers at the man by the warehouse door.

To Deb's relief, the flunky turned and unlocked the door. The warehouse swallowed him up and then spit him back out several minutes later. In his wake, an older black man was carrying Bobby in his arms. He must've been the one who'd impersonated Robert.

Deb willed her feet to stay planted on the ground. She still had her weapon pointed at Zendaris and she couldn't lose that advantage. "What's wrong with him?"

The man holding him answered. "Just sleeping. He's okay."

"Wake him up."

The man shook Bobby a little and said a few words. Bobby popped his head up and shifted his arms and legs.

She blew out a breath. "Put him down and let him come to me."

"Wait." Zendaris held up his hand. "I'm the one giving the orders. You're still holding a gun on me and I don't have the plans. You could grab your son and shoot me."

"Your men have guns on me." She shrugged. "If I shot you, they'd shoot me or Bobby. I'm not going to risk that."

"Sort of a Mexican standoff here, eh?" He snapped his fingers at the man. "Put him down. I want my plans."

The man put Bobby on the ground, and Bobby blinked and rubbed his eyes. With her gun still on Zendaris, she called to her son. "Bobby, it's Mommy. Come to me."

"Mommy!" His little feet slapped the ground as he ran toward her. He threw himself at her legs, wrapping his arms around them. She wanted nothing more than to pick him up in her arms, but this farce wasn't over yet.

Zendaris held out his hand. "The plans. Or I really will have my men shoot both you and your son before you can even get a shot off."

Something whizzed through the air and Zendaris's mouth hung open.

This is it. Deb took a step back.

A form hurtled from behind the Dumpster. Beau yelled, "Get down, Deb."

In one motion, he swept Bobby from the ground and wrapped his arms around both of them as he tackled them. Deb heard more whizzing noises above them. A car started, and then stalled.

Beau dragged her and Bobby a few more feet away from the chaos, his body still covering theirs.

He looked over his shoulder from the ground. "How many? How many men does he have with him?"

"Zendaris."

"Down."

"Driver."

"Down." He spoke into the mic clipped to his jacket, and she realized he wasn't talking just to her.

"Man who had Bobby."

Deb overheard a voice coming through Beau's earpiece. "He ran back into the warehouse. J.D., launch the smoke bombs."

Deb screamed over the new noise and tried to cover Bobby's ears. "My escort."

"Down."

Cade—it must've been Cade—replied, "I got someone exiting the gate."

Someone else shouted, "All clear, all clear."

Beau spoke into his mic. "Verify. Verify the all-clear."

Nobody answered. The connections had been lost.

Black smoke poured from the warehouse and

Deb squeezed her eyes shut. It was over. The nightmare was finally over.

"Zendaris not down, not out."

Gasping, Deb lifted her head and Beau sat up to face Zendaris's weapon pointed at them.

Zendaris was propped up against the car, the open door serving as a shield from any incoming bullets. But there wouldn't be any incoming bullets because the other three had thought the drama was over and had left their posts.

He pointed at Beau. "Who the hell are you?"

"Just a curious bystander."

"Another Prospero robot, most likely. Do you really have those plans, Deb?"

"Yes." The gun Deb had been holding on Zendaris before all hell broke loose was gouging her hip. She shifted toward Beau to push it in his direction. "The plans are in the car, but you'll never get away with them. My Prospero brothers will be here in seconds."

"Maybe they will, but I'm going to take a few of you down before I go, starting with you."

Her gun flashed before her as Beau swung it free while throwing himself in front of her and Bobby. Two shots echoed in the night and Bobby whimpered in her arms.

Beau rolled from her body and crouched beside her. "Are you okay?"

She struggled to a sitting position, pulling

Bobby into her lap. Touching Beau's face, she whispered, "Are you?"

"I am now." He pointed the gun at Zendaris's body, coiled on the ground.

"What the hell happened?" Gage ran toward Zendaris and kicked the gun from his hand. "How did he survive that shot to the heart?"

Beau rose to his feet and extended his hand to Deb. "Bulletproof vest. Your shot knocked him down, maybe even knocked the wind out of him, but his vest saved him."

"Damn fedora. Couldn't get a clean shot at his head."

J.D. and Cade had arrived, too, picking through the weapons and trying to ID the men. "That's gotta be everybody."

Deb stroked Bobby's face. "Are you okay, my love?"

He nodded. "Where were you, Mommy?"

"I was trying to get you home."

Beau touched a finger to Bobby's nose. "Didn't you know, Bobby? Your mom is Superwoman."

Epilogue

The light breeze caused a ripple through the meadow of Colorado wildflowers, and the bride resembled another flower as she floated along the edge of the meadow, her white skirt billowing behind her.

Deb sipped champagne, and the bubbles tickled her throat. "Let's go congratulate the bride and groom."

She grabbed Bobby's hand and rested her fingers on Beau's arm. The crowed parted for him as he led her to J.D. and J.D.'s new wife, Noelle. Crowds would always part for Loki.

Deb kissed Noelle on the cheek and hugged J.D. "This is it, cowboy. You're a married man. Are you going to put down roots in Colorado?"

"We'll probably go back to D.C. at first. This is Noelle's brother's place. We've just been helping him out." He kissed his wife's hand.

"It's beautiful."

Like a magnet, their little group drew the

others. Gage, looking like a *GQ* model, approached with a dark-haired beauty—Zendaris's former nanny.

Cade, with his beachy-blonde wife by his side and their little boy skipping in front of them, joined them as well.

Deb studied each of their faces. Even though Robert was gone, she still had a family. These men were her brothers, and she knew now she could trust them with her life and her son's life. She should've realized that before.

They stood silent for a moment, consciously aware for a split second that they shared a special bond—not just the Prospero Team Three agents, but the people they loved. The people Zendaris had targeted. They stood frozen, as if drinking in the beauty and inhaling the freedom of the moment.

Then they all began to talk at once.

Cade clinked his glass with Deb's. "I guess we owe Zendaris for leading Deb straight to the anti-drone plans. Dr. Herndon was probably ready to put them back on the market."

"Now the Defense Department has them." J.D. draped his arm around his bride's shoulder.

Gage snorted. "Better the DOD than the CIA. You should've seen that compound the Agency had down in Panama."

"This is a wedding. Enough shop talk." Cade's

wife, Jenna, ruffled Bobby's hair and smiled at Deb. "He's so cute. Is he better now?"

"He's getting stronger every day, thanks to his dad." Deb brushed her hand across Beau's back.

He caught her hand and kissed her fingers before going back to his conversation with Gage's girlfriend, Randi, about Colombia.

Jenna's son, Gavin, pulled on his mom's arm. "I wanna run over there, Mommy. We can see horses."

Jenna put her finger to her lips. "Just a minute, Gavin. Deb, is it okay if I take Bobby with us? I don't know about your little guy, but mine's just itching to get his fancy clothes dirty."

Deb crouched next to Bobby. "Do you want to go with Gavin and his mommy to see the horses?"

"Can Daddy come?"

"He'll come in a minute. Go play with Gavin."

Jenna took both boys by the hand and called after Cade to join them.

J.D. and Noelle peeled away from the group to dance with their new in-laws, and Gage pulled Randi into the wildflowers where they disappeared from view.

Beau jerked his chin toward Bobby with the Starks. "He looks good, huh?"

"Looks good, feels good. The transfusions worked like a charm." She hitched her arms around Beau's neck and kissed his chin. "He's so happy to have his daddy in his life—we both are."

"And his daddy is happy to be there. He fit right in with the cousins, didn't he?"

"Your family is completely turning his head. He's already clamoring for ten brothers and sisters."

He dragged her close and whispered in her ear in a way that still gave her shivers, "Should we get started on that request?"

"We can work on it, but let's wait a few years before actually creating another perfect child. You're seriously considering Jack's offer to join Prospero, aren't you?"

"I am if he'll have me."

She kissed him. "I'm giving you a very good recommendation."

"Thanks, babe. That'll go far because you know about all of Loki's exploits, don't you?"

"I don't want to know about *all* of them." She put a finger on his yummy lips that she couldn't stop kissing.

"Really? Because I have one I don't think I told you about before."

"Watch yourself."

"Did I ever tell you about the one where I was in this bar in Zurich?"

She tilted her head to one side. "Hmm, I don't think so."

"So, I was in this bar in Zurich, relaxing after a particularly perilous assignment."

"Fascinating."

"I looked across the room and my eyes locked onto the most intriguing woman I'd ever seen in my life."

"She sounds dangerous."

"You have no idea."

"What happened? Did she turn out to be a double agent? Lead you on a high-speed chase through the mountains?"

"Something much scarier than that." He traced her lips with his fingertip. "She made me fall in love with her."

* * * * *

LARGER-PRINT BOOKS!
GET 2 FREE LARGER-PRINT NOVELS PLUS
2 FREE GIFTS!

◆ HARLEQUIN®

INTRIGUE®

BREATHTAKING ROMANTIC SUSPENSE

HILPI3R

LARGER-PRINT BOOKS!

**GET 2 FREE
LARGER-PRINT NOVELS
PLUS 2 FREE
MYSTERY GIFTS**

Love Inspired®

SUSPENSE

RIVETING INSPIRATIONAL ROMANCE

Larger-print novels are now available...

YES! Please send me 2 FREE LARGER-PRINT Love Inspired® Suspense novels and my 2 FREE mystery gifts (gifts are worth about $10). After receiving them, if I don't wish to receive any more books, I can return the shipping statement marked "cancel." If I don't cancel, I will receive 4 brand-new novels every month and be billed just $5.24 per book in the U.S. or $5.74 per book in Canada. That's a savings of at least 23% off the cover price. It's quite a bargain! Shipping and handling is just 50¢ per book in the U.S. and 75¢ per book in Canada.* I understand that accepting the 2 free books and gifts places me under no obligation to buy anything. I can always return a shipment and cancel at any time. Even if I never buy another book, the two free books and gifts are mine to keep forever.

110/310 IDN F5CC

Name	(PLEASE PRINT)	
Address		Apt. #
City	State/Prov.	Zip/Postal Code

Signature (if under 18, a parent or guardian must sign)

**Mail to the Harlequin® Reader Service:
IN U.S.A.:** P.O. Box 1867, Buffalo, NY 14240-1867
IN CANADA: P.O. Box 609, Fort Erie, Ontario L2A 5X3

**Are you a current subscriber to Love Inspired Suspense books
and want to receive the larger-print edition?
Call 1-800-873-8635 or visit www.ReaderService.com.**

* Terms and prices subject to change without notice. Prices do not include applicable taxes. Sales tax applicable in N.Y. Canadian residents will be charged applicable taxes. Offer not valid in Quebec. This offer is limited to one order per household. Not valid for current subscribers to Love Inspired Suspense larger-print books. All orders subject to credit approval. Credit or debit balances in a customer's account(s) may be offset by any other outstanding balance owed by or to the customer. Please allow 4 to 6 weeks for delivery. Offer available while quantities last.

Your Privacy—The Harlequin® Reader Service is committed to protecting your privacy. Our Privacy Policy is available online at www.ReaderService.com or upon request from the Harlequin Reader Service.

We make a portion of our mailing list available to reputable third parties that offer products we believe may interest you. If you prefer that we not exchange your name with third parties, or if you wish to clarify or modify your communication preferences, please visit us at www.ReaderService.com/consumerschoice or write to us at Harlequin Reader Service Preference Service, P.O. Box 9062, Buffalo, NY 14269. Include your complete name and address.

LISLPDIR13R

ReaderService.com

Manage your account online!

- Review your order history
- Manage your payments
- Update your address

We've designed the Harlequin® Reader Service website just for you.

Enjoy all the features!

- Reader excerpts from any series
- Respond to mailings and special monthly offers
- Discover new series available to you
- Browse the Bonus Bucks catalog
- Share your feedback

Visit us at:

ReaderService.com